SITUATION HILARIOUS, BUT SERIOUS

"You're telling me that Joe wants to drop Sabrina for you?" Frank asked in disbelief. "What did he say?"

"He told me he's always had a thing for girl drummers," Eddie said. "And he's always had a thing for long curly blond hair. So all of a sudden I'm everything he ever wanted."

"Get real," Frank said.

"Hey, to quote him exactly, he said, 'Baby, you really make my bell ring.'"

"What's he gonna do next?" Frank asked.

"I don't know," Eddie replied. "All I know is I ain't hanging around to find out."

"Wait," Frank said. "You can't leave now."

Eddie stared at Frank and shook his head. "Forget it, Frank. I don't care whether this fits into your plans for Sabrina or not. I don't care about nothing except gettin' outta here before Sharkbait Joe decides to give me a great big kiss."

ROCK 'N' ROLL SUMMER

The Boys in the Band

Playing for Love

by Todd Strasser

ROCK 'N' ROLL SUMMER

The BOYS in the BAND

Todd Strasser

HarperPaperbacks
A Division of HarperCollinsPublishers

HarperPaperbacks *A Division of* HarperCollins*Publishers*
10 East 53rd Street, New York, N.Y. 10022

Front cover photograph by Retna Ltd./Jenny Acheson
Back cover photograph by Retna Ltd./Caroline Summers

First printing: July 1996

Printed in the United States of America

HarperPaperbacks and colophon are trademarks of HarperCollins*Publishers*

❖ 10 9 8 7 6 5 4 3 2 1

To Joanna Lewis Cole
with fond appreciation

ROCK 'N' ROLL SUMMER

The BOYS in the BAND

ON THE SIDEWALK IN FRONT OF Sound Machine Music Studios, Frank Strone, 17, beheld a vision of beauty. She was reclining in the passenger seat of a shiny new black Jeep, which was double-parked across the street. Her face was angled toward the sun, and her wavy auburn hair fell past her bare shoulders. Tiny beads of perspiration collected on her small, slightly upturned nose and above her upper lip. Her skin was unblemished and bronzed. She was wearing a pink bikini top and cutoff jeans. Her tanned arms were thin and her legs were long and slim.

Frank suddenly found it hard to breath. It might have been the heat, but he had a feeling it was the *girl*. She was . . . magnificent.

But who was she? Frank had never seen her before in town. That probably meant that she wasn't from around there. Which meant that she might be leaving soon. Which meant that he better meet her before she left.

A hand clapped down on his shoulder. "Uh, Frank?"

Frank turned to his buddy, Eddie Falco. Eddie was short and squat, built like a fire hydrant. A red bandanna was pulled tight over his head like a bathing cap. Sweat darkened the lower edge of the bandanna where it crossed Eddie's brow. Perspiration ran crookedly from his temples down over the day-old black stubble on his jaw.

"What are we gonna do?" Eddie asked.

"About what?" Frank asked, distracted by the girl in the Jeep. He watched as she hooked her finger through her hair and pulled it back, revealing a long, slender neck. Frank stared at her wrists and hands. They were small and elegant. He felt something stir inside him. She must have been a goddess . . . or a mirage. She looked like one of those girls from a music video. Too beautiful to be real.

Who was she?

What was she doing in Clotsburg?

"About what?" Eddie repeated, eyebrows rising in surprise. He reached up and tapped Frank on the head. "You here, Frank? Hello? Anyone home? I'm talkin' about this summer. About having no band, no gigs, and no money."

Frank watched the girl in the Jeep shift positions. She picked up a pair of sunglasses from the dashboard and put them on, then studied herself in the side view mirror. The Jeep was parked outside Rudy's Bar and Grill, a small brick-face joint with a large glass window and a couple of neon beer signs. The girl glanced at the pub's darkened front window as she tucked a long slim leg up under her chin. She looked a little impatient.

Frank knew this was an opportunity he couldn't let pass. He'd never forgive himself if he didn't find out who she was. Besides, who-ever had left her sitting out in the hot sun wasn't being very considerate. Frank stepped into the street. It was so hot the asphalt felt sticky under his shoes. The bright sun ham-mered down on him, making him squint.

"Hey!" Eddie called behind him. "Where're you going?"

"I'm just gonna talk to someone," Frank called back. It felt even hotter in the street than it did on the sidewalk. He was about halfway across when she noticed him. Not that he could see her eyes under the sunglasses, but he could tell she was watching by the way she cocked her head and shifted in the seat again. Frank walked up to the Jeep and leaned on the driver's side door. The shiny black metal practically scalded his arm, but he hardly felt it. His heart was banging nervously, but she couldn't see that. The car had red seats and smelled new.

"Hi." He brushed his long straight brown hair out of his eyes and smiled.

"Hi." She regarded him uncertainly from behind the shades.

"Kind of hot," Frank said.

"Uh huh."

He could see she was the cautious type, a little shy and nervous with strangers. He liked that. The bold, pushy ones turned him off.

"How come you're not at the beach?" Frank asked.

"Oh, I don't know." She glanced across the sidewalk at Rudy's Bar again.

"Waiting for someone?" Frank asked.

"I guess." She didn't sound real enthusiastic.

"Wasn't very nice of him to leave you out here in the sun," Frank said.

"How'd you know it was a him?" she asked.

"A girl wouldn't pick this color," Frank said, gesturing to the Jeep. "Not that I mean to sound sexist or anything, but a girl would pick white or light green. Something like that."

She smiled slightly, revealing an even row of bright white teeth. Maybe she was a model or an actress or something.

"Think you'll go to the beach tomorrow?" Frank asked.

"I don't know."

"I bet you really want to, but he hates it," Frank guessed. "He hates the sand and the heat, and he hates wearing a bathing suit because he doesn't want anyone to see his scrawny legs."

The girl tipped down her sunglasses and stared at him with a surprised, amused expression. Just as Frank had imagined, she had beautiful dark eyes.

"How . . . ?" She started to ask, then caught herself and laughed. "You're funny."

"I'm right, huh?" Frank felt his eyes lock onto hers.

"Maybe."

Eddie waved from across the street. "Jeez, Frank, come on!"

Frank looked back at him. "In a second."

"Sounds like you have somewhere to go, Frank," she said, pushing the sunglasses back up over her eyes again.

"It can wait," Frank said. "By the way, now that you know my name, what's yours?"

"Are you always this pushy?" she asked in a playful tone.

She was right. Frank knew he was pushing too hard. Normally, even if he was interested in a girl he didn't show it. But right now he had to gamble. Otherwise, he might never see her again.

"No, I'm not usually like this," he said. "But I'd really like to know your name."

She shook her head. "My mother told me never to talk to strangers."

"You always listen to your mother?"

"No."

They both grinned.

"I bet it's something beautiful," Frank said. "Like a flower or something. Like Heather or Lily or Tulip."

"Tulip?" She laughed again. He liked her laugh.

"Marigold?" Frank guessed.

"Sabrina."

"Sabrina," Frank repeated. "I've never met a Sabrina before."

"I bet you say that to all the Sabrinas." She winked.

"Hey, how'd you know?"

They gave each other knowing smiles. It felt like they'd met somewhere before. Like they'd known each other a long time; had been kidding around with each other for years. There was an instant connection Frank had never felt before. Like they were perfectly tuned.

"Hey, Frank!" Eddie called again. "Come on!"

"Your friend sounds impatient," Sabrina said.

"He's always impatient," Frank said. "So, uh, you're not from around here, are you?"

"Not that far away."

"What brings you to Clotsburg?"

Sabrina glanced toward the bar again. Frank looked more closely at the darkened front window. Inside he could see a guy with a shaved head, wearing a leather vest with no shirt underneath. Tattoos of skulls and dragons decorated the pasty white skin of his biceps.

"*Sharkbait Joe?*" Frank could hear the shock in his own voice.

Sabrina frowned. "Sharkbait?"

"Yeah, that's what they call him," Frank said.

"He never told me that," Sabrina said.

"How long have you known him?" Frank asked.

"Not long."

That was no surprise. Inside the bar, Sharkbait Joe wiped his mouth on his arm. Frank and he had never been formally introduced, but like everyone else in Clotsburg, Frank knew he was a total dirtbag. *Worse* than a dirtbag. He dealt drugs and was rumored to have killed a guy in a fight. A girl like Sabrina couldn't be with *him*. It wasn't possible.

"What are you doing with that . . . er, with Joe?" Frank asked.

"He's—" Sabrina's answer was interrupted by the loud bang of a door flying open as Sharkbait Joe stormed out of the bar, heading straight for Frank. He was shorter than Frank, and scrawny, but muscular at the same time. A ragged scar zigzagged under his right eye. An earring of a cross hung from his left ear.

He was followed by a big guy with unkempt greasy hair and a blue polo shirt with holes in it stretched to the limit by his big belly. Grungy Arnie, one of Sharkbait Joe's goons.

"Mind if I ask what you're doin'?" Sharkbait Joe stopped just inches from Frank. He had a cigarette stuck behind his ear, and his breath smelled of beer. His teeth were brown and twisted.

"Just talking." Frank stood his ground.

"What about?"

"About what she's doing here," Frank replied.

"She's with me." Joe grabbed the door of the Jeep and yanked it open. It banged into Frank's arm, but he didn't budge. Joe couldn't get in the Jeep. Normally Frank never messed with idiots like Joe, but now he was stuck. He couldn't let this jerk back him down in front of Sabrina.

"I'd move if I was you," Joe sneered.

"Most people say excuse me," Frank replied.

Sharkbait Joe squinted daggers at Frank. Out of the corner of his eye, Frank saw Eddie cross the street and stop a few yards away.

"Uh, Frank?" Eddie said nervously. "You know who that is, right? I really think we ought to go."

Once again, Sharkbait Joe swung the door into Frank, who still didn't budge. Frank felt a little sick inside. It was obvious what this was going to lead to.

"I said move," Joe growled.

"Make me."

Frank felt Eddie's hand go around his arm. "I really think you should do what he says, Frank."

Frank stood his ground. His eyes stayed locked on Joe's. It was daylight. They were in the middle of Main Street in Clotsburg; there were witnesses everywhere. Joe wouldn't do anything stupid. He might have been crazy, but Frank had a feeling he wasn't *that* crazy. Behind Joe, Grungy Arnie stepped forward.

Joe waved him back. "I'll take care of this twerp."

He reached into his pocket and pulled out something black. Holding it up in front of Frank's face, he pressed a button and a pointed silver blade popped out and glinted in the sunlight for all to see.

Frank swallowed. On second thought, maybe Sharkbait Joe *was* that crazy.

"Look!" Eddie suddenly shouted. "The cops!"

As soon as Joe turned to look, Frank swung his hand forward, slapping the knife out of Joe's grasp. As it clattered to the street, Grungy Arnie lunged forward, his big arms outstretched to get Frank in a bear hug. Frank ducked under his grasp and punched the big tub in the stomach.

"Oooff!" Arnie doubled over and fell to his knees.

"I don't see no cops," Sharkbait Joe growled and bent down to get the knife.

"Frank, we gotta get out of here!" Eddie yanked on Frank's arm, pulling him away.

Frank looked at Sabrina as he backpedaled. Once again their eyes locked. He hated leaving her. "See you around okay?"

Eyes wide with surprise, Sabrina nodded.

Grungy Arnie was getting off his knees. Sharkbait Joe was coming at them with the knife. Frank and Eddie turned and ran.

2

***"ARE YOU INSANE!?"* EDDIE MOANED.** He was slumped down in a tattered yellow overstuffed chair in the middle of Frank's room. Frank pulled open a window and turned on the fan. The room was actually the attic of a three-story house in a residential part of Clotsburg. Frank's mom rented the third floor and the attic. The sloping ceiling was covered with posters of rock guitarists. CDs and music magazines were scattered around the floor.

"Want a drink?" Frank went over to the half-refrigerator he kept up there so he didn't have to go down to the kitchen and see his mother all the time.

"Sure." Eddie pulled the bandanna off his head and used it to wipe the sweat off his face. "Flirting with death tends to make me thirsty."

Frank pulled a cold two-liter bottle of Coke out of the fridge and handed it to him. "I wasn't flirting with death."

"You don't think Sharkbait Joe would have used that knife?" Eddie took a big gulp and wiped his mouth on the back of his hand. Eddie was an unusually hairy guy for a seventeen year old. He had a full chest of hair, hairy arms, and hair on his back. He had to shave every morning, and sometimes again at night if he had a big date.

"I wasn't gonna hang around to see." Frank got the bottle back and took a gulp himself.

Eddie got up and aimed the fan so it blew in his face. Then he slumped down in the chair again. Frank had found the chair in the street.

"Jeez, it must be a thousand degrees up here," Eddie muttered.

"At least." Frank smiled. Eddie's exaggerations always amused him.

Eddie reached for the bottle of Coke again and took another gulp. "And what was it all about anyway? Who was that girl? You know her?"

Frank shook his head.

"You risked your life for some girl you don't even know?" Eddie asked, amazed.

Frank nodded. "She could be the one, Eddie."

"What?"

"The one."

"The one? What are you talking about? Which one?"

"The one I've been looking for, dude."

Eddie looked at him like he was crazy. "Let me ask you something, Frank. If she's the girl you've been looking for all your life, how come she's hangin' around with an amoeba like Sharkbait Joe?"

That was bothering Frank too. If she was the kind of girl he imagined she was, she wouldn't go near a guy like Joe. But Frank was almost certain she *was* what he thought she was. So it was a mystery. He shrugged. "I know it doesn't make sense. I just got this feeling. She's a nice girl."

"Well, she may be nice and she may be the one," said Eddie, "but she ain't the one for you, okay? She's Sharkbait Joe's and unless you wanna risk serious mutilation, you won't go near her."

Frank sat down on his amp and wiped his forehead on the sleeve of his T-shirt. It felt like an oven up there, and it wasn't even July yet. "Maybe you're right, Eddie, but I wouldn't mind seeing her again."

Eddie stared at him. "What's wrong with you? I've never seen you act like this in your life. Usually girls are crawling all over you and you could care less."

"They weren't Sabrina."

"Sabrina?"

"That's her name."

"So you talked to this girl for all of about ten seconds and suddenly you think she's it? She's the one you're gonna die for?"

Frank shrugged. He just had that feeling. Like she was a definite potential. But who really knew?

"It must be the heat." Eddie leaned forward and stuck his face right in front of the fan. He pulled his sweat-soaked T-shirt away from his body. "Look at me. I'm sitting in front of the fan doing nothing and I'm still sweating bullets."

Frank picked up his Stratocaster and fingered some riffs. The unamplified strings made tinny sounds.

Rap . . . rap. Someone knocked on the door.

"Yeah?" Frank said.

The door opened and a thin guy dressed in a black T-shirt and jeans came in. His name was Richie Palomino and he was Frank's and Eddie's manager. Richie was rail thin, with thick curly hair pulled back into a ponytail. He had graduated high school the year before, which made him only two years older than Frank and Eddie.

Richie was a nice guy, but he wasn't much of a manager. In fact, it often seemed to Frank that what Richie lacked in experience, he made up for with ineptitude. But Eddie insisted he was better than no manager at all.

Richie winced as he stepped into the room. "You got the heat on or something?"

"Frank likes it hot," Eddie said. "So you got some good news for us?"

Richie shook his head and took a swig from the bottle of Coke. "I got nothing. There's no work. All the clubs around here are usin' DJs for the summer. You wanna play live music, you gotta go to the shore."

"Thanks, Richie," Eddie said irritably. "Now tell us something we *don't* know."

Richie slid his hands into his back pockets. "Too bad you guys ain't girls. You know Sam Zuckert from the city?"

Eddie and Frank shook their heads.

"Zuckert promotes packaged concepts," Richie said.

Eddie screwed up his face. "Talk in English, Richie."

"He comes up with a concept, then he packages it. If it works, he promotes it. If it develops a following, he signs it."

"If it itches, does he scratch it?" Frank asked.

"Huh?" Richie frowned.

Eddie nudged Frank in the ribs. "Can it, wiseguy." Then he turned back to Richie. "What's all that got to do with us not being girls?"

"I read in the trades that Zuckert wants to put together some all-girl bands to play the shore clubs this summer," Richie said. "If any of them click, he's gonna get behind them in a big way. Like with gigs at places like Trax in the city, and an album contract and all that. They're gonna start auditioning girls next week."

"Great," Eddie grumbled. "I'll call my doctor and have a sex change operation tomorrow."

Richie shrugged. "What can I tell you, Eddie? You and Frank are my two favorite players, but I can't make miracles."

"So what're we supposed to do all summer?" Eddie asked.

"Get a job?" Richie said.

A softball bat was lying in the corner of Frank's room. Eddie jumped out of the chair and grabbed it. He moved toward Richie, holding the bat threateningly.

"Get a job!" he shouted. "Did you say, *get a job? Don't ever say that!*"

Richie backed away with his hands in the air. "Jeez, Eddie, what's with you?"

"What's with me?" Eddie yelled. "We hired you to get us gigs and all you can do is tell us to get a job? Like I need you for this?"

Richie backed toward the door. "Look, I'm sorry okay? What can I tell you? If you guys were girls, you'd have it made."

"*If we were girls?*" Eddie shouted, raising the bat higher. "Get outa here!"

Richie pulled open the door. "You know, I don't deserve this from you guys. I'm bustin' my butt and this is what I get?"

"Get out!" Eddie swung the bat.

Bang! Richie slammed the door behind him. Eddie slumped back into the yellow chair with the bat across his lap.

"If we were girls," he muttered shaking his head as he slapped the head of the bat against his palm.

"Forget him, Eddie," Frank said. "The guy's a joke."

Eddie just shook his head and kept slapping the bat against his hand. "I just can't believe it, Frank. I can't believe I'm gonna spend another summer in this ghost town while a bunch of girl bands get to play clubs all up and down the shore."

"You could always put on a skirt, Eddie," Frank joked.

"Yeah." Eddie grinned.

Frank grinned.

Then Eddie stopped grinning. He straightened up in the chair.

Clunk! The bat fell to the floor. "That's it!" Eddie gasped.

"What's it?" Frank asked.

Eddie stared up at him. "You gotta do it, Frank."

"Do what, Eddie?"

Eddie got to his feet and started to pace around, looking very excited. "It's the opportunity of a lifetime, Frank! It may be the last shot we'll ever get!"

"Last shot at what?" Frank asked. He didn't know what his friend was talking about.

"Wait here!" Eddie ran out of the room.

3

A COUPLE OF MINUTES PASSED before Eddie came back, carrying a small brown paper bag.

"Come with me," he said, crossing the room.

"Where?" Frank asked.

"Outside."

The next thing Frank knew, Eddie moved the fan from the window. Then he climbed out onto the lower part of the roof where it was flat and covered with black tar paper. Frank got up and stuck his head out the window. Eddie was standing on the roof with an egg in his hand.

"You wanna see your summer?" Eddie asked. "*This* is gonna be your summer."

Kneeling down on the black roof with the egg in his hand, Eddie pulled a drumstick out of his back pocket and cracked the shell. The egg spilled out onto the hot tar shingles.

"You feeling okay, Eddie?" Frank bent over and climbed out the window into the blazing hot sun. He wiped his brow with his blue bandanna. It must've been a hundred and twenty degrees out there.

"No, I'm not feeling okay," Eddie said. "You wanna know why? Because you wanna spend another summer in this wasteland, sweating your butt off while everyone we know is at the beach."

"Not everyone we know."

"Well, everyone we *should* know," Eddie countered. "Anyone who stays here for the summer is a total loser, and that includes us."

Frank sighed and felt a bead of sweat run out of his hair and down his temple. He wondered if Eddie was losing his marbles.

"There, you see?" Eddie pointed down at the egg, which had turned slightly white. "It cooked."

"It's not cooked," Frank replied. "The bottom turned white, that's all. And what's this all about, anyway?"

"I'm telling you it's cooked," Eddie insisted.

"Look, Eddie, get to the point already," Frank said.

"You don't believe it's cooked?" Eddie asked. "Okay, I'll eat it."

He started back across the roof to the window.

"Eddie, you don't have to eat an egg off my roof to prove to me it's gonna be a hot summer," Frank said.

"Yeah, I do," Eddie said. "Know why? Cause for the first time in our lives we got a chance to get into a band that's gonna get gigs,

Frank. A band that's gonna make real money and maybe even get a shot at the big time. A band that's gonna spend the whole summer at the beach . . . And *you're* not gonna want to do it!"

"What are you talking about?" Frank asked.

"The band Richie told us about."

"The all-girl band?"

"Right."

"We're not girls, Eddie."

Eddie glared at him and then ducked through the open window.

"Where're you going?" Frank asked.

"I need a knife and fork."

Eddie disappeared back into Frank's room. The guy had gone certifiably psycho. Frank gazed around at the rooftops of the stores and houses that lined the street below. The flag over the World War I monument in the square drooped lifelessly. The grass had turned brown. A thin gray haze hung motionless in the air. It was so hot that even the pigeons had disappeared. The sun beat down on Frank's long brown hair, making his scalp feel tight. What was he doing up on the roof with an egg?

The curtain inside the window rustled and Eddie started to climb back out. He had a knife and fork in his hand.

"You've gone psycho, Eddie," Frank said.

"I'm psycho?" Eddie asked. "You're the one who doesn't want to spend the summer at the shore and *I'm* psycho? I think you got it backward, bud."

"I never said I didn't want to go to the shore,"

Frank said. "But we've got no money, no jobs, and no place to stay."

Eddie kneeled down and poked the fork into the yoke. The yoke broke and began to spread over the egg white. Eddie sliced the egg in two with the knife.

"The pigeons sit on this roof, Eddie," Frank cautioned.

"Oh, yeah?" Eddie raised an eyebrow. "Well, good. Maybe they've left some seasoning." He managed to get some of the drippy egg white onto the fork and lifted it toward his mouth.

Frank watched in utter disbelief. "You really want to go to the shore that bad?"

"Let me put it to you this way," Eddie said. "I spend another summer in this town, I guarantee you I'm a serial killer come September."

Frank took a deep breath of hot air. "Okay, we'll go to the shore. We'll sleep under the boardwalk or something."

"No, we'll stay in motels, man. We'll be right on the beach. We'll be in a band."

"How?"

"This is the 90s, Frank. We can fake it."

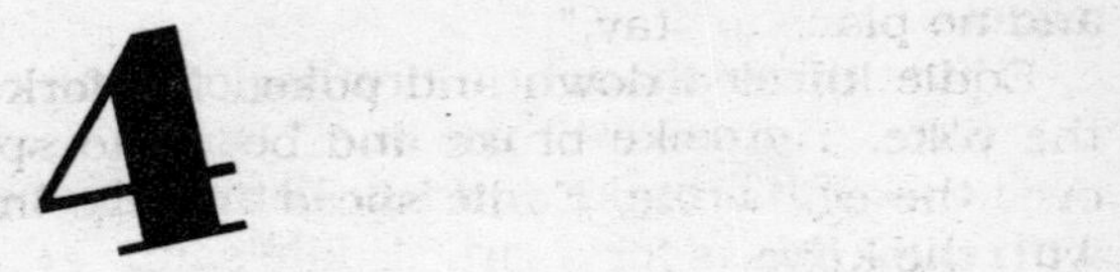

"YOU GUYS ARE, LIKE, REALLY SICK," Donna said, cracking her gum.

Donna was Eddie's fifteen-year-old sister. Eddie and Frank were in her bedroom. Posters of nearly naked sweaty rock stars hung on the walls, but the bed was covered with furry pink and green stuffed animals. Music was playing on the CD player, and on the TV was that soap opera *Days of Our Lives.* Donna had about six hoops in each ear and brown hair that went straight up from her forehead and added about six inches to her height. She was two years younger than Eddie.

"Yeah, I know, Donna," Eddie said. "You've told us that about six thousand times already."

Eddie was sitting in a chair at Donna's makeup table. He was looking at himself in a mirror that was lined with bare light bulbs. Eddie was wearing pancake makeup, eye shadow, mascara, lipstick, and a big blond wig.

Donna was rubbing a little blush into his cheeks.

"I just never thought a brother of mine would . . . like . . . cross over the line," Donna said.

"Look, if it'll make you feel better, the reason I'm doing this is for a girl," Eddie said.

"Wow, she must be, like, really sick, too," his sister said.

"She's not gonna see me like this, butt brain," Eddie said irritably. "I'm gonna take all this stuff off when I see her."

"So who is she?" Donna asked.

"I don't know yet," Eddie said. "But I'm gonna meet her at the beach. We're gonna splash in the waves together and play in the sand and—"

"Share makeup tips," Donna added.

"Drop dead."

Frank was sitting on Donna's bed, reading *Tiger Beat*. When he looked up, he couldn't believe what he was seeing. With that big blond wig and all that makeup, Eddie actually looked like a girl. At least, he looked like a girl from the neck up. From the neck down he still looked like a small fullback.

"Is that you, Eddie?" Frank teased him.

"Believe it, dude," Eddie said, staring at himself in the mirror. "I almost look good."

"Don't get carried away," Donna muttered.

"You're gonna teach me how to put all this junk on myself?" Eddie asked her.

"Or you and Frank can put it on each other," Donna said.

Frank winced at the thought of him and Eddie putting makeup on each other. It was crazy.

Meanwhile, Eddie stood up from the chair. "Your turn, Frank."

But Frank didn't move from his seat on the bed.

"Come on, dude," Eddie said.

"I'm having my doubts about this, Eddie," Frank said.

"Remember, Frank," said Eddie. "This is our ticket outta here. It may even be our ticket to fame and fortune."

"Or a psycho ward," Donna added.

"She's right, Eddie," Frank said. "This is ridiculous."

"Staying in Clotsburg is ridiculous," Eddie said. "Look, Frank, you wanna waste this summer melting in your attic, go ahead. You wanna blow it dreaming about this girl, Sabrina, who you don't even know, fine with me. But think about the beach, dude. Imagine boogie boarding through those cool blue waves. Think about having cookouts at night and girls in string bikinis."

"As long as they're not us," Frank said, winking at Donna.

"I can just see you guys in bikinis." Donna shook her head and groaned.

"Just give it a try," Eddie said. "Maybe you'll even like it."

Frank kept staring at Eddie. It was eerie. Donna had done an amazing job. His friend could actually pass for a girl.

"Look, I'm just asking you to *try* it," Eddie urged him.

Frank shook his head. "You can get dressed up like a girl. Not me."

"Hey, Donna, you think Frank's gonna need as much makeup as me?" Eddie asked. "I mean, he's already got long hair. His face is pretty smooth. I'll bet he could get away without hardly anything."

"No one would need as much makeup as you," Donna said.

"That's not the point," said Frank.

"Okay, look," Eddie said. "I wasn't gonna drop this low, but you give me no choice. I saved your life today, Frank. I mean, if it wasn't for me, Sharkbait Joe would've left a permanent crease in that handsome face of yours. Now all I'm asking is you try this. I mean, personally, I think it's the *least* you could do."

Frank knew Eddie had a point. "Okay, I'll try a little makeup. Just for you, Eddie. But that's it." He walked reluctantly over to the chair and sat down. What the hell, anything was worth a try.

Donna smiled at him. "You're gonna be fun to do, Frank."

"How come he was fun and not me?" Eddie asked.

"Because *he's* good-looking," Donna said, running her fingers through Frank's long straight hair.

"Jeez, from my own sister." Eddie shook his head.

Donna started to rub some concealer onto Frank's face.

"You sure this stuff comes off?" Frank asked.

"With soap and water," Donna said. "I'll take you guys to the store and we'll buy all the stuff."

"How come you're being so nice to us?" Frank asked her.

"You kidding? I'm lookin' at a chance to get rid of my dirtbag brother for the whole summer."

"Hey, what do you think of this?" Eddie asked from across the room, where he'd pulled on one of Donna's bras across his T-shirt.

"Get that off right now!" Donna shouted. "You're gonna stretch it!"

"Chill out," Eddie shot back. "I didn't even hook it."

"You probably don't know how," Donna said.

"Hey, believe me," Eddie said. "I've got plenty of experience unhooking bras."

"Yeah, right." Donna winked at Frank.

"Seriously," Eddie said. "You got some bras that'll fit me and Frank?"

"I'm not giving you guys my bras," Donna said. "You can go buy your own."

The thought of wearing a bra was too much for Frank. He started to get up out of the chair.

"Hey, where're you going?" Eddie asked.

"Sorry, Eddie, as much as I'd like to spend the summer at the shore, I can't go through with this."

Eddie jumped in front of him and clutched his shirt. "Okay, so you won't show me any gratitude for saving your life. Do I have to beg you? Do I have to get down on my knees? This is the last free summer I'll ever have for the rest of my life, Frank. Do you understand what that means? Next year I'll graduate high school and my parents'll make me get a job."

Tears actually welled up in Eddie's mascaraed eyes. Frank stared at him in shock. Eddie blinked and the tears ran down his cheeks. He turned to Donna.

"If I cry, will I ruin it?"

"Naw, it's waterproof," his sister said.

Eddie turned back to Frank. "Don't do this to me, Frank. Please, I'm begging you. Let's try to get out of here this summer. Let's try to have a life before it's too late!"

Eddie started blubbering again. Frank couldn't standing watching his friend cry.

"Okay, okay, I'll do it if you promise to stop crying."

Eddie instantly grinned. As Frank sat down on the chair again, Eddie patted him on the shoulder. "Believe me, Frank, this could turn out to be the greatest summer we ever had."

AUDITIONS STARTED AT 4:00 P.M. At 3:30 Frank parked his mother's car across the street from the Sound Machine Studios. Eddie was sitting next to him. In the backseat were two green garment bags with girl's clothes and makeup kits in them.

"Ready?" Eddie asked in a high-pitched girl's voice he'd been practicing all week.

"I guess," Frank said.

"Not like that," Eddie said.

"I guess," Frank repeated, this time in the high-pitched voice Eddie had been making him use.

"We have to talk like girls, Frankie, or it's not going to work," Eddie said.

Behind the steering wheel, Frank nodded reluctantly. He took a deep breath and let it out slowly. He'd done a lot of crazy things in his life. But nothing compared to this. Why had he gone along with this ridiculous idea? Mostly it was the incredibly hot weather and Eddie's constant mixture of nagging and promises that the shore would be paradise. Besides, there'd been no sign of Sabrina since the day they'd had that run-in with Sharkbait Joe.

"You can't chicken out on me now," Eddie said in his girl voice.

Frank looked down at the steering wheel and shook his head. "It's not gonna work, Eddie."

"Don't give me that," Eddie said impatiently switching back to his regular voice. "You promised you'd do it. I learned how to do the makeup. I borrowed money from my sister to buy these stupid clothes. You back out now, I swear I'll kill you."

"We can't pretend to be girls," Frank said. "I mean, we might be able to get away with it for a couple of days. Maybe even a week. But sooner or later they'll figure it out."

"Okay, okay," Eddie said, chewing on a thumbnail. "Maybe they will. But in the meantime, we'll be at the shore. During the day we'll look for jobs and a place to live. By the time they figure out we're not girls, maybe we'll have other things lined up."

Frank stared at him. "I've never seen you like this."

"Look, I've explained it to you a million times," Eddie said. "I wanna have a life before high school's over because once it's over I ain't gonna have a life, I'm just gonna have a job."

"Maybe we'll have a band," Frank said.

Eddie glared at him. "Sure, you and me, bud. We're gonna be the next superstars. Dream on."

"It happens."

"Look, Frank, I don't want to talk about it," Eddie snapped. "All I ever wanted in life was to be a drummer, but there are ten thousand guys out there just like me. Know how many are gonna make it big? Twenty? Thirty? All I want is to have a good time this summer so someday when I got three kids and a wife I can look back and remember that one summer when I really had fun."

Frank turned and looked across the street at the front doors of the Sound Machine Studios. It was located in an old movie house that still had its movie marquee. A short girl with black spiky hair and black clothes went in carrying a guitar case.

"They're starting to go in." Eddie reached into the backseat to pull out the garment bags. "Come on, we gotta go."

Frank didn't move from behind the wheel. He hated to let Eddie down, but he knew he couldn't go through with it. It was one thing to try on makeup in Donna's room, but go out in public that way? No way . . . It just wasn't that important to him. Sure, he'd like to spend the summer at the shore. Who wouldn't? But dress up like a girl to be in some all-girl band? Forget it.

Besides, he kept thinking about Sabrina. So maybe he hadn't seen her around all week. Maybe if he hung around he'd see her *next* week.

"Frank?" Eddie had gotten out of the car. He was standing on the sidewalk with the garment bags.

Frank shook his head. "Sorry, Eddie." He turned the key in the ignition and started the car's engine.

"What are you doing!?" Eddie looked in the car window.

"I'm going," Frank said. "I'm sorry, man. If you really want to do it, you should. But I can't."

"You can't do this to me," Eddie gasped desperately. "I can't go in there alone."

"Yeah, you can," Frank said.

"Don't do it, Frank." Eddie started to get excited. "I'm begging you, man. Don't do this!"

Frank could tell Eddie was going to throw a fit. He couldn't blame him, but he didn't have to hang around and watch it, either. "Later, bud."

He put the car in drive and hit the gas, keeping an eye on Eddie to make sure the guy didn't do anything crazy like jump on the trunk.

Screech! Tires screeched loudly on his left.

CRUNCH! The car shook and lurched. Frank knew he'd hit another car. He looked up through the window into a familiar face in the other car. A beautiful girl with wavy auburn hair was staring back at him with a shocked expression.

Sabrina!

Frank blinked. What was she doing there? Frank focused on the other car, which met his at the front bumper, forming a V. It was a black Jeep.

Uh-oh . . .

A door slammed and Sharkbait Joe stomped

around to the front of the Jeep to inspect the damage. From Frank's point of view inside the car, it didn't look too bad. His mother's car was already so banged up she probably wouldn't even notice. But Sharkbait's Jeep was scraped pretty bad. Frank slid across the seat and got out on the passenger side. He stared across the car's roof at Sabrina. He couldn't take his eyes off her.

"Uh, hi," he said.

"Hello again." Sabrina managed a weak smile. Then she glanced nervously at Joe.

For a second Frank forgot everything that had just happened. She was there again, sitting in the Jeep looking as beautiful as she had the first time he'd seen her. His insides started to feel mushy. It was so unlike anything he'd ever felt before.

Then a voice said, "You again?"

Frank turned and saw that Sharkbait Joe was glaring at him. Joe's eyes narrowed and he reached into his vest and pulled out his knife.

"Run, Frank!" Eddie yelled.

"*I'll kill you!*" Sharkbait Joe screamed and started climbing over the cars toward Frank. Grungy Arnie jumped out of the back of the Jeep and joined him.

Frank started to run. Eddie raced ahead of him, the two garment bags flapping at his sides. They ran down the sidewalk and turned down an alley lined with smelly garbage cans and dumpsters. At the end of the alley was an old green dumpster, and behind it, a chain-link fence. Eddie threw the garment bags over the fence, then he and Frank climbed up on the dumpster and vaulted over.

On the other side of the fence, Eddie picked up the garment bags. He and Frank ran down another alley behind some buildings.

"Hey, in here!" Eddie yanked open a dented metal door and they ducked inside a dimly lit vestibule. Eddie pushed the door closed behind them. The air in the vestibule was hot and stale. Frank's heart beat like a drum as he gasped for breath.

Eddie was panting. Sweat poured down his face. "Shh!" He brought his fingers to his lips and they both listened.

Outside they heard nothing.

"I think we lost 'em," Eddie whispered. Frank reached for the doorknob, but Eddie grabbed his arm. "What are you doing? They're probably still out there."

"Then what're we gonna do?" Frank asked, looking around the vestibule. Graffiti was scrawled over the walls, and phone numbers were scratched into the door.

Eddie looked down at the garment bags. Frank knew what he was thinking.

"Forget it, Eddie."

"You go back out there lookin' like you, and Sharkbait Joe's gonna slice you into Wonder Bread," Eddie warned.

Suddenly they heard a blast of electric guitar coming from somewhere in the building. Frank looked at a wooden door on the other side of the vestibule. "Where are we, Eddie?"

"Uh, I don't know."

But Frank always knew when Eddie played dumb. He opened the wooden door a crack and found himself peeking out onto a stage. A couple of girls were hooking up electric guitars. A bunch more were hanging around in the seats beyond the stage. It looked like the inside of an old movie house.

"Amazing," Eddie whispered. "We must've gone in the back way to the Sound Machine."

"Yeah, amazing." Frank smirked as he let the door close. "So now that we're here, I bet you want to dress up and audition, right?"

"Well . . . " Eddie sort of nodded.

"Forget it."

Suddenly, the knob on the metal door that led outside started to turn.

"It's them!" Eddie hissed. He quickly reached down and slid a security bolt into a hole in the floor. Outside someone pushed on the door, but the security bolt held it closed. Frank pressed his ear to the door.

"They gotta be around here somewhere." It was Grungy Arnie.

"I'm gonna kill that guy." Sharkbait Joe was seething. "I'm gonna slice him into nuggets."

"Okay, Frank," Eddie whispered, pointing at the door. "You wanna go back out and say hello? I bet they'll be really glad to see you."

Frank knew he was stuck. There was no way they could go back out there. Then he looked down at the garment bags and had an idea.

"All right, Eddie, I'll get dressed up like a girl. But *not* to audition. Just to sneak out of here."

TWENTY MINUTES LATER EDDIE HAD put on makeup, the blond wig, and a long-sleeve purple blouse buttoned up to the neck. Frank was wearing a black Danskin under a loose T-shirt. They were both wearing padded bras. Frank felt like someone had tightened a belt around his chest. How did girls wear these things? And what was the deal with the straps? One kept sliding off his shoulder, the other was so tight that it felt like it was digging right into the shoulder muscle.

Loud rock music was coming from the other side of the wooden door that led to the stage. They could hear a girl singing. Eddie pushed open the door a little. "Frank!" he whispered hoarsely.

"What?" Frank hissed, reaching under the T-shirt and trying to adjust the bra straps.

"You gotta see this!"

Frank looked over Eddie's shoulder and

through the door. He could see a couple of studio musicians on the stage, backing a singer with long, wavy auburn hair. The studio was dark except for some spotlights on the girl.

"It's her!" Eddie whispered.

He was right. Sabrina was standing at a microphone, singing. She must have been auditioning. *That's* why she'd been in Sharkbait Joe's Jeep.

"Not exactly a nightingale," Eddie whispered.

He was right again. Sabrina's voice was okay, nothing great. They watched as a preppy-looking guy joined her on stage. The guy had short brown hair and wire-rim glasses. He was wearing khaki slacks, a light blue shirt with the sleeves rolled up, and a tie.

"Who's that?" Eddie whispered.

"Must be the guy who's in charge of the audition," Frank whispered back.

"Okay, thanks, that was terrific," the preppy guy said, clapping his hands without enthusiasm. "Next."

"But I hardly had a chance to get warmed up," Sabrina said.

"Believe me, I heard enough," the preppy guy replied.

Frank watched Sabrina shrug and walk off the stage. A new girl with blond hair got up behind the microphone.

Eddie turned to Frank. "So what do you want to do?"

There was only one thing Frank wanted to do. He wanted to go in there. He wanted to find

Sabrina. He wanted to make sure he never lost sight of her again.

"Go in," he whispered.

Instead of going through the door, Eddie stared at Frank's chest and frowned.

"What's wrong?" Frank asked.

"They're crooked."

"Huh?" Frank looked down. Eddie was right. The left one was up near his shoulder, the other was down near the edge of his rib cage.

"Now, Frank, you're never to let anyone do this except me," Eddie said, imitating someone's mother. He grabbed Frank's fake appendages and straightened them.

"There, that's much better," Eddie said, smiling maternally. "Now remember, we gotta talk like girls."

"Right," Frank replied in a girl voice.

They went through the door and cut through the back of the stage and into the darkened theater. There must've been fifty girls out there in the seats waiting to audition. As they walked up the aisle, Frank kept looking for Sabrina, but she was nowhere in sight.

They stopped by the doors at the back of the studio. The blond girl was singing on the stage.

"Where's Sabrina?" Frank whispered, trying to peer around in the dark.

"Where's the preppy guy?" Eddie whispered back.

Suddenly, they heard grunts coming from outside the doors.

"*Ooof—Ugh . . . unh . . .* "

It sounded like someone was getting the crap

knocked out of them. Eddie peeked out the door. "Uh-oh, look."

Out in the hall, Sharkbait Joe and Grungy Arnie had backed the preppy guy against the wall. The preppy guy was doubled over and holding his stomach. Sharkbait was whispering something in the preppy guy's ear. The preppy guy was nodding. Sabrina was still nowhere in sight.

"What's that all about?" Frank whispered to Eddie.

"I think Sabrina just got the singing job," Eddie whispered back.

Sharkbait Joe stepped back and let the preppy guy straighten up. The preppy guy's face was red and he was grimacing. He straightened his clothes and started back toward the studio. Eddie and Frank quickly backed away from the doors and slid into two seats in the shadows. The preppy guy walked back into the studio and toward the stage, interrupting the blond girl who was trying out.

"Thanks, that was really great," he said.

"But I didn't get to finish," the blond girl protested.

"I heard all I had to hear," the preppy guy replied.

"See?" Eddie whispered. "I told you Sabrina got the job."

The preppy guy turned toward the audience. "Okay, we're gonna start trying out drummers now. Any drummers here?"

All at once, Frank realized the perfect way to stay close to Sabrina. He nudged Eddie. "Go, dude."

Eddie gave him a shocked look. "What are you talking about? I thought we were sneaking out."

"I just changed my mind," Frank said. "We gotta get into this band."

"You serious?"

"Knock 'em dead."

"All right!" Eddie grinned. He got up and started to bound down the aisle.

"Hey!" Frank hissed.

Eddie stopped and turned. "What?"

"You're a girl, remember?"

"Oh, yeah." Eddie started down the aisle again, trying to walk daintily. He joined two other girls waiting in front of the stage. The girls regarded Eddie coldly. The preppy guy looked down from the stage at Eddie and sort of grimaced.

"Okay, you each get three minutes to show your stuff," the preppy guy said. "Just tell the boys up here what you want to play. They know all the songs."

The preppy guy came down from the stage and sat down in the seats with someone. Frank couldn't tell who the other person was because it was dark and he could only see the back of the person's head. He got up and moved down to a seat in the row behind the two guys.

The two girls went first. Both were competent drummers. Frank leaned forward and listened as the preppy guy and the other one exchanged comments.

"They're okay," the preppy guy said. "I was hoping for someone with a bigger sound."

"Well, if you want my advice, you better pick one of 'em," the other person said.

Frank's eyes widened with shock. It was Richie, his manager! He must've been managing some of these girls too.

"What about that blonde?" the preppy guy asked, gesturing to Eddie.

"Forget it," Richie said in a low voice. "First of all, she ain't exactly attractive. The thing about a girl band is it ain't just about music. It's about looking good too."

"Not this time," the preppy guy said. "Sam wants the best band he can find."

"Well, I know all the players around here," Richie said. "I never seen her before. I don't know who she is, but I can guarantee you she ain't any good."

"Well, let's give her a shot," the preppy guy said. He waved at Eddie. "It's your turn, sweetheart."

"Oh, thank you," Eddie said sweetly.

As Eddie walked up on the stage and settled behind the drum set, the studio musicians gave each other snide looks.

"You gotta be kidding," someone behind Frank whispered.

"Not a chance," whispered someone else. "I don't care if she drums like Keith Moon."

Eddie started drumming. The bass drum boomed, cymbals crashed, drumsticks bounced off the skins and flew high in the air. Eddie would catch them without a missed beat. Onstage the studio musicians looked shocked, then got into it. The jam went well beyond three minutes.

Frank only wished he could see Richie's and the preppy guy's faces.

When Eddie's tryout ended, he jumped up from the drum set and gave the studio musicians high fives. The preppy guy turned to Richie.

"I thought you knew all the players around here," he said with a smirk.

"She must be from out of town," Richie whispered back.

"Well, that's just the sound we need," the preppy guy said.

"But my girls are a lot better-looking," Richie protested.

"Doesn't matter," said the preppy guy. "She'll be behind the band. No one'll see her."

"EVERYONE HERE?" BRIAN SHOUTED.

Brian was the preppy-looking guy with the short brown hair and the wire-rim glasses. He'd just graduated from the Yale School of Management and had gotten a job with Sam Zuckert's organization in the city. Managing the Femme Brigade was his first job. The Femme Brigade was the name of the band.

It was ten o'clock in the morning and they were sitting in one of those long vans bands often travel in. They were parked on Main Street, Clotsburg, outside Sal's Pizza. Besides Frank, who'd been hired to play lead guitar, and Eddie, there was Chrissy, the waif-like lead singer with the surprisingly big voice; Ann, the tall, dark-haired bass player; Rachel, the redhead who played keyboards; and Toni, a shapely black girl who wore low-cut dresses and shared the backup singing with Sabrina. The back of the van was filled with instruments, amps, and sound equipment. Space was pretty cramped.

"Everyone except Sabrina as usual," Toni muttered, pointing out the van's window.

Frank looked out the van's window. Sabrina was outside on the sidewalk with that dirtbag Sharkbait Joe. Frank hadn't seen her since the day of the auditions. But now he hoped he'd see a lot of her. Brian was moving the band to a motel down on the shore to practice without "outside distractions" and keep an eye on what the competition was up to. The rehearsals would be closed to outsiders and the girls would only be allowed to see their boyfriends at meals and for few hours in the evening.

Outside on the curb, Sharkbait Joe and Sabrina had tilted their heads toward each other. Sharkbait Joe was talking to her in a low voice Frank couldn't hear. Sabrina was nodding.

Eddie, who was now known as Ellie, was sitting next to Frank. They were both wearing their girl disguises. He leaned over and whispered, "Every time I see that guy, it gives me the creeps."

"Hopefully we won't be seeing much of him from now on," Frank whispered back.

They watched Brian climb off the van and approach the two. "Okay, Sabrina, time to go."

Sharkbait Joe glowered at him. "When I'm through."

Brian immediately backed off. "Right, of course, I'll wait as long as you want."

In the van, the girls watched this.

"How did that guy ever get a job managing a rock-and-roll band?" Toni groaned, rolling her eyes.

"Hey, he graduated from Yale," Eddie said, disguising his voice as Ellie.

"So?" Toni asked, "what's *that* got to do with anything?"

"Forget him," said Ann, the tall black-haired girl. "What I want to know is, what's Sabrina doing with a creep like Joe?"

"Love is blind," Chrissy, the lead singer, said with a sigh.

"Well, if that's the case, Sabrina would be better off with a seeing-eye dog," Toni cracked.

The girls laughed. Outside, Sabrina and Sharkbait Joe were still engaged in their tête-à-tête. Brian climbed back into the van and sat in the driver's seat.

"Hey, Brian," Toni yelled, "how come we gotta squeeze in here with all the equipment? Couldn't you just rent two vans?"

"You know what it costs to rent two vans, Toni?" Brian replied.

"Well, if we gotta sit in here, then come on," said Toni. "Let's get this show on the road."

"Uh, in a moment," Brian said.

"You gonna let that skinny hood push you around?" Toni asked.

Brian turned and glared at her. "Mind your own business, Toni."

"Whoa," Toni said. "I think I touched a sore spot."

Outside, Sabrina and Joe appeared to be finishing up. Frank had an idea.

"Move," he whispered to Eddie.

"What?" Eddie whispered back.

"I said, move," Frank hissed. "Find another seat. Sabrina's gonna need a place to sit."

"And I don't?" Eddie whispered.

"Sit with one of the other girls," Frank whispered.

"Are you serious?" Eddie asked in a low voice. "What if they want to talk about makeup or bodily functions or something?"

"Better get used to it," Frank whispered. Outside, Sharkbait Joe gave Sabrina a pretty modest peck on the cheek. Frank gave Eddie a nudge. Eddie got up and looked around. Toni was sitting in the seat behind them, wearing one of her low-cut dresses and showing a lot of leg. Eddie sat down next to her.

Toni stared down at his lap. Eddie looked down and realized she was looking at his hands. They were hairy. He quickly slid them together between his legs.

Toni shook her head and looked away. Eddie just grinned nervously and stared straight ahead. Meanwhile, Sabrina climbed into the van. Frank smiled up at her and pointed to the seat next to him. Sabrina smiled weakly back at him and sat down.

Brian put the van into gear, and it lurched away from the curb. "Okay, everyone, listen up," he said as he started to drive. "There are seven girls in the band and you have to share three rooms. That means three girls in one room and two girls each in the other two rooms. I don't really care how you divide up, so you figure it out."

"Rachel, Chrissy, and I will share the room for three," Ann, the tall, dark-haired bass player said. Frank had noticed that those three seemed pretty tight. No doubt they were friends from before.

"Okay," said Brian. "Then it's up to you other four to decide how you want to divide up."

The next thing Frank knew, Sabrina gave him a curious look. But before he could say anything, he heard Toni in the seat behind him ask Eddie if he wanted to be roomies.

Eddie glanced at her low-cut dress. "Uh, sure."

Frank couldn't believe it! He twisted around in his seat and gave Eddie a look.

"Oh, uh, I forgot," Eddie stammered in his fake girl's voice. "I already told Frank I'd room with him."

"Frank?" Toni made a face. "Frank who?"

"Oh, I meant, Frankie," Eddie quickly said. "We've know each other since first grade."

"Whew." Toni shook her head. "Something tells me you two were *made* for each other." Now she reached forward and tapped Sabrina on the shoulder. "How about you, beautiful? Want to share a room?"

"Sure," Sabrina said. "That would be great."

Now that the living arrangements had been agreed to, Frank settled more comfortably into the seat. Sabrina glanced at him again and smiled weakly. Just her smile made his heart start to quiver. All he wanted to do was take her in his arms and run away to someplace where Sharkbait Joe would never find them.

"Excited?" Frank asked in his fake girl's voice.

Sabrina bit her lip. "Scared is more like it."

Frank pretended to be surprised. "Scared of what?"

"Singing," Sabrina said. "I mean, I've always dreamed of being a singer in a band, but now that it's really happening . . ." She shook her head in wonder.

"Hey, I heard you at the audition," Frank said. "You'll be fine."

"You think?" Sabrina asked hopefully. "Oh, you don't know how much it means to me to hear someone say that."

The next thing Frank knew, Sabrina leaned close to him. Their shoulders pressed together, and she started to whisper in his ear. Frank felt a shiver run down his right side.

"I really didn't think Brian liked my singing," she whispered. "In fact, I was totally shocked when he told me I was in the band."

So, she had no idea that Sharkbait Joe had made certain she'd be in the band. Yeah, that made sense to Frank. If she'd known what Sharkbait had done, she wouldn't have gone along with it. He could tell she was a girl with scruples.

"Well, he must've liked you," he said. "You're in the band."

"Have you ever been in a band before?" Sabrina asked.

"Oh, yeah." Frank smiled. His lips felt funny because they were coated with lipstick. "Ever since junior high I've been in and out of them."

"What's it like?" Sabrina asked.

"Well, if you do it right, it's really a lot of work," Frank said in his girl voice. "There's so much to get used to. We not only have to learn the songs. We have to learn each other's styles too. We have to try to get really tight musically. That, er, means that it's really best to try to forget about the rest of your life and just focus on the band."

"That won't be too hard for me," Sabrina said. "What about you, Frankie. Do you, uh, have a boyfriend?"

"Me!" Caught off guard, Frank acted surprised. Then he remembered he was a girl. "Oh, uh, there's someone, but it's nothing serious."

"Is that your choice or his choice?" Sabrina asked.

Frank let out a dainty sigh. "Neither. We just met. We don't really know each other that well yet. But every time we see each other, it's, you know, like instant attraction."

Sabrina nodded and gazed out the window. They were on the highway now.

"I, uh, noticed that you have a boyfriend," Frank said.

"Hmmmm." Sabrina didn't sound exactly enthusiastic.

"Do you think you'll see him a lot at the shore?" Frank asked.

"He has a friend with a house nearby," Sabrina said. "I have a feeling he'll be around."

Darn, Frank thought. Then he said, "You don't sound very excited."

Sabrina shrugged. "It's one of those things that's hard to explain."

"Want to try?" Frank asked.

"Not right now," Sabrina said. "Maybe someday when we know each other better."

Right, Frank thought. Hopefully that would be someday soon.

THE MOTEL WAS IN THE MIDDLE OF nowhere and looked like something out of a horror movie. The dirt parking lot was filled with potholes and weeds. The screen doors were torn, the curtains were tattered, and the some of the windows were broken. There was a fenced-in area with a pool, but the gate was locked and the pool was dry and cracked.

"I thought you said we were going to stay at a motel on the beach," Toni said as the van rolled into the parking lot.

"Do you know what a motel on the beach costs?" Brian asked as he parked the van outside the motel office. "Besides, all we're going to do for the next two weeks is rehearse."

"Aren't we going to get to go to the beach?" Ann asked.

"Sure, at some point," Brian said. He got out of the van and went into the office. A few moments later he came out with the room keys.

"Okay, girls," he said. "Time to unpack."

"Tell me again about frolicking in the waves," Frank whispered as he and Eddie carried their bags toward their room.

"Look, that's what I imagined, okay?" Eddie whispered back. "How was I supposed to know Brian would be so cheap?"

"The beach must be five miles from here," Frank whispered. They stopped outside their room. All the rooms faced the parking lot. Two doors down, Sabrina and Toni stopped outside their room. Frank gave Sabrina a little smile and a wave.

"Now this is what I call luxury accommodations," Eddie cracked as he pushed open the door and carried his suitcase in. Frank followed behind him and closed the door. The room had two single beds with orange covers, a couple of cheap brown dressers, and a TV that looked like it was from ancient times. The carpeting might have once been beige, but it was so stained that it was hard to be sure.

"Better make sure it's locked," Eddie said, and flopped down on the bed. He pulled off his blond wig. "Jeez, I never knew a wig could be so hot. I feel like I'm wearing a fur hat!"

Frank slid the chain across the door. "Better keep your voice down," he said. "These walls look pretty thin to me."

Eddie sat up on the side of the bed and pulled his T-shirt off and unhooked his bra. The straps had left impressions on his hairy chest and shoulders. "And this thing, man. It's so constricting!"

"Now you know why women don't like to wear

them all the time," Frank said, looking around. Everything—the carpeting, bed covers, furniture, and window sills—was covered with cigarette burns.

"I don't know about this, Frank," Eddie said, shaking his head. "Maybe you were right. It ain't easy being a girl. Maybe we should blow this off before we get in too deep."

Frank stared at his buddy in disbelief. "I know I didn't hear you right. This was *your* idea, Eddie. You were the one who said you were gonna go crazy if we spent another summer in Clotsburg. You were the one who wanted to go to the shore in a girl's band."

"Yeah, but this ain't the shore," Eddie said. "This is the middle of nowhere."

"Well, look," Frank said. "We made a commitment. I think we have to stick with it."

"Geez, Frank, you know what life is gonna be like if we stay with this band?" Eddie asked. "Wearin' these clothes everyday. Puttin' all this makeup on everyday. Wearin' this wig. What're you gonna do when the girls want to go to the beach, huh?"

"I'll say I'm allergic to the sun," Frank said. He opened the bathroom door and went inside. The bathroom smelled of mildew. The tiles around the bathtub were covered with some kind of dark green scum. Through a small screened window over the toilet he could see out behind the motel—a wasteland of tall grass surrounding a rusting school bus.

"And how about when some guy starts hitting on you?" Eddie asked.

"I'll hit back," Frank said with a grin as he came back out of the bathroom.

"Very funny." Eddie smirked. "Look, we both know this is all about Sabrina. Have you figured out what this is gonna lead to? I mean, you think she's gonna fall in love with you *as a girl*?"

"Look, I don't know what's gonna happen," Frank said. "All I know is this is the only way I can stay close to her. And right now that's all I want out of life."

Eddie stared at him in disbelief. "Man, I don't know what's gotten into you. I've never seen you act this way for a girl. This sure ain't the Frank Strone I've know since first grade. Man, you never acted like this for a girl before."

"There's never been a girl like this before, Eddie," Frank said. "I keep telling you, this is a once-in-a-lifetime thing."

"And like I keep telling you," Eddie said. "You better be real careful because if Sharkbait Joe finds out, it's gonna be one *short* lifetime."

Rap . . . rap . . . Someone knocked on the door.

"Who's . . . " Frank started to ask in a male voice, then caught himself and switched to a female one. "Who's there?"

"Hey, Frankie, Ellie, I have to talk to you."

Frank turned back to Eddie. "It's Brian!"

Eddie put his hands on his shaved head. "Oh, crap, man!"

"Get the wig and clothes and go in the bathroom!" Frank whispered. Then he turned to the door and said in his girl voice. "Just a minute, Brian. We're not decent."

Eddie grabbed his stuff and hurried into the bathroom, slamming the door closed behind him. Frank checked himself in the mirror and then opened the door.

"Thanks, Frankie." Brian came in and looked around. "Where's Ellie?"

"I'm in here," Eddie called from the bathroom in his girl voice.

"Okay, listen up," Brian said. "In half an hour we're getting together for our first rehearsal."

"Where?" Frank asked.

"Uh, a place nearby," Brian replied vaguely.

"What kind of place?" Frank asked.

"Uh, well, it's a storage locker."

"A what?" Frank frowned.

"One of those places where people store stuff," Brian said. "I rented us a locker. It's pretty quiet in the summer, you know? And the great thing about it is we can lock it up at night and not have to worry about dragging all the equipment back—"

Brian stopped talking and stared at something lying on the bed. Frank followed his eyes. It was Eddie's padded bra! Frank quickly reached over and grabbed it, hiding it behind his back.

"That yours?" Brian asked.

"No, it's Ellie's," Frank said.

Brian glanced at the bathroom door. "Geez, that's too bad."

Frank knew he had to change the conversation fast. "Well, rehearsing in a storage locker sounds . . . er, interesting."

"And we've got a lot of work to do," Brian said. "We're here to rehearse. Our first gig's in two weeks and you girls have to get up there and look professional."

Eddie poked his head out of the bathroom. He was wearing his blond wig again. "Are you implying that we're not professional?" he asked in his girl voice.

"Well, you two are," Brian said. "A couple of the others, I'm not so sure about. But that reminds me of something, Ellie. Now I know this is going to sound rather personal, but I'm just trying to be realistic. Being in a band isn't just about playing good. It's about looking good too, know what I mean? It sure wouldn't hurt if you dropped a few pounds."

"What about Frankie?" Eddie asked.

Brian glanced at Frank. "You look okay, Frankie. Except for those hands. You must have the biggest hands I've ever seen on a girl."

Frank looked down at his hands and back at Brian. "That's why I play guitar."

"Well, maybe you could do something with them," Brian said. "Like put on some nail polish or something. Anything that'll pretty them up."

"Okay," Frank said.

Brian headed back for the door. "So you have half an hour to get unpacked and ready. Then we meet at the van and go over to rehearse."

Brian went out. Frank got up and locked the door behind him. Eddie came out of the bathroom.

"Sexist pig," he muttered.

Frank threw Eddie's padded bra at him. "Look what you left on the bed."

Eddie caught the bra. "Brian see it?"

Frank nodded.

"What'd he say?" Eddie asked.

"He said it was too bad," Frank said.

Eddie frowned. "Too bad? What's *that* supposed to mean?"

"It means that it's too bad that you're fat and ugly *and* you got no chest," Frank said with a grin.

Eddie glared at the door Brian had just gone through. "Oh, yeah? Well, look who's talking."

"But he ain't a girl, Eddie," Frank said.

"Well, if he was, he'd be a lot uglier than me," Eddie said.

"Right," Frank said, turning to his suitcase. "Anyway, you heard what he said. We got half an hour to unpack and then we got our first rehearsal in a storage locker."

"Yeah, yeah," Eddie said. "Just what I always dreamed of."

As they unpacked their suitcases and put their clothes away, Frank began to notice that the motel room was starting to fill with a somewhat unpleasant scent. Finally he stopped and stared at Eddie.

"What?" Eddie asked.

Now Frank noticed something else. The thick black stubble on Eddie's chin was starting to show through his makeup.

"Didn't you shave and shower this morning?" Frank asked.

Eddie stopped. "Well, actually I didn't have

time. See I slept late. Wait a minute, how'd you know?"

"Because you got chin stubble sprouting through your makeup, and this room is starting to smell like a pig sty," Frank said. "Your better get in the bathroom and take a shower."

"Geez." Shaking his head, Eddie went into the bathroom and ran a shower. A little while later he came out with a towel wrapped around his waist. His chin was covered with shaving cream and he was carrying a razor.

"Can't you shave in the bathroom?" Frank asked.

"Naw, the mirror's all steamed up," Eddie said. "I can't see a thing."

He walked over to the mirror above the dresser and started to shave.

Rap . . . rap . . . Suddenly there was a knock on the door.

"Uh, who is it?" Frank asked in his girl voice.

"Toni and Sabrina," came the reply. "Open up."

Frank spun around to Eddie and jerked his head toward the bathroom.

"Geez, man," Eddie muttered, "I'm gettin' tired of you telling me to get in the bathroom."

"Just get in there," Frank hissed, checking his makeup in the mirror. Eddie headed back into the bathroom.

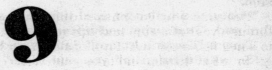

THIS TIME FRANK MADE SURE EDDIE had taken everything with him, then he opened the door. Toni came in, followed by Sabrina. Toni was wearing another one of her tight, low-cut dresses. Sabrina was wearing jeans and an oversize white oxford shirt.

"Great digs, huh, Frankie?" Toni asked, sitting down on Frank's bed.

"It's all right," Frank said in his girl voice while smiling at Sabrina.

"So where's your other half?" Toni asked.

"I'm in here," Eddie's girl voice called from the bathroom.

"You get a visit from Brian before?" Toni asked.

"Yes."

"He told Sabrina he wanted her to wear tighter clothes," Toni said.

"Really?" Frank said. It sounded like a great idea to him.

Sabrina blushed slightly. "It's really not my style."

"Honey, you better get used to looking sexy," Toni said. "That's what backup singers are *for.*"

"I guess I'll wear a leotard," Sabrina said.

"So what'd Brian tell you and Ellie?" Toni asked.

"He told Ellie she should lose some weight," Frank said in his girl voice.

"Who does he think he is?" Toni huffed. "And what did he tell you, Frankie?"

"Uh, he told me I should do something about my hands," Frank said.

"Here, let me see," said Sabrina.

The next thing Frank knew, Sabrina took his hand in hers and ran her fingers lightly over it. Frank could smell her perfume again. It took all his willpower not to take her in his arms.

"Well, they are a little rough," Sabrina said.

"And big," Frank said in his girl voice. "It's just the way I was born."

"My mom owns a beauty salon," Sabrina said. "I used to work there sometimes after school. I can probably do something with the cuticles. How about tonight after rehearsals?"

"Oh, uh, what about your friend?" Frank asked.

"Joe? He said he had some business to take care of," Sabrina said. "He said he wouldn't be coming down for a few days."

"Well, in *that* case . . . " Frank couldn't believe his luck. Sharkbait Joe wasn't going to be around for a few days, and he and Sabrina were getting together that night!

Rap . . . rap . . . Someone knocked on the door. "Okay, girls!" Brian shouted from outside. "Time to go."

Frank turned back to the bathroom. "Oh, Ellie," he said in his girl voice. "Time to shake a leg!"

"Here I come." The bathroom door swung open and Eddie came out wearing his blond wig, a long sleeved turtleneck, and jeans. Frank immediately noticed that Sabrina and Toni were giving him strange looks.

Frank looked closer. Oh, no! Eddie had left some of the shaving cream near his ears!

"Ellie, dear, I think you better check yourself in the mirror," Frank said.

"Huh?" Eddie frowned and then went over to the mirror over the dresser and looked into it. Then he quickly wiped away the white foam.

Meanwhile, Toni nudged Frank and whispered. "Is it my imagination, or was that shaving cream?"

"It's a glandular problem," Frank whispered back. "Not enough hormones."

Toni and Sabrina nodded gravely.

"The poor thing," Sabrina whispered.

"We try not to make a big deal about it," Frank whispered back.

Eddie turned away from the mirror and came toward them. "Okay, girls," he said in a chirpy voice, "let's get this show on the road."

The storage locker was about the size of a small garage. There was no air-conditioning and it was stifling inside. Brian had to make frequent runs to a nearby grocery store for cold drinks. The rehearsal lasted all day. Then they broke for dinner and went back to play for another three hours. By the time they finished, everyone was exhausted. They climbed back onto the van and slumped into their seats. By now it was pretty obvious to Frank that Chrissy, Ann, and Rachel intended to stick to themselves, leaving him and Eddie with Sabrina and Toni.

"It's a good thing we finally stopped," Eddie said in his girl voice. "My hands were starting to cramp up terribly."

"You're lucky it was just your hands," Toni groaned.

"Why?" Eddie asked.

Toni gave him a look. "Don't you ever get any *other* cramps, honey?"

Eddie frowned and glanced at Frank, who quickly whispered in his ear.

"Oh!" Eddie's eyes widened. "Oh, of course! How silly of me to forget! Oh, yes, aren't those just the worst? Thank God, it's only once a month."

Toni was still giving him a funny look. But then she nodded and turned to Sabrina. "My throat's raw," she said. "How about yours, Sabrina?"

Sabrina nodded. She was sitting with Frank again and gave him a questioning look.

"The tips of my fingers are all calloused," Frank said in his girl voice. "But when I play for a long time I can feel blisters start to develop under them."

Brian climbed onto the van and got into the driver's seat. "Okay, everyone, that was a good first day. If we keep working that hard we'll be halfway ready for our first gig in a couple of weeks. Now I know everyone must be tired, so let's make it an early night. We've got another long day of rehearsals tomorrow, and the day after that too."

"Aren't we getting any time off?" Toni asked.

"Believe me, Toni, if we're not ready for our first gig in two weeks, you'll get *plenty* of time off," Brian replied. "Like the rest of your life."

Brian turned around and started to drive the van. In the back, Toni slumped down in her seat.

"Oh, man," she muttered. "And I thought being in a band was supposed to be glamorous."

They rode back to the motel in the dark. Sitting next to Sabrina, Frank couldn't believe how close he was to her, and yet so far away at the same time. The temptation to run his fingers through her long beautiful auburn hair was so great he had to fight himself from doing it.

"So how'd you like your first day of rehearsals?" he asked in his girl voice.

Sabrina shrugged a little. "It was okay."

"You don't seem real excited," Frank said.

"Oh, I am," Sabrina said. "I guess I just didn't expect it to be so hard. Singing so much and trying to hit all those notes and remembering what to do when."

"That's what rehearsals are all about," Frank

said. "Believe me, at the rate we're going, in two weeks you'll be able to do this in your sleep."

"But won't that take the fun out of it, Frankie?" Sabrina asked.

"It will until you do it in front of a live audience," Frank said. "Then it's a whole different story."

Sabrina smiled at him.

"What?" Frank asked.

"I don't know, Frankie," Sabrina said. "You're just so . . . experienced. You've done so much. I feel like such a . . . kid next to you."

"Just wait," Frank said.

The van pulled into the motel parking lot.

"Okay, everyone, it's bedtime," Brian said. "I want you girls fresh and rested in the morning."

"Aye, aye, captain." Toni saluted him and the other girls chuckled.

Toni and Sabrina, and Frank and Eddie went into their respective rooms. As usual, Eddie pulled off his wig and flopped down on the bed.

"Whew, what a day!" he gasped. "That Brian's turned into a real slave driver."

"So what'd you think of the band?" Frank asked.

"It feels good to be playin' again, man," Eddie said. "It's a good group. That Chrissy can really sing, and Rachel and Ann know what they're doing. Sabrina seems a little stiff though. I gotta feeling she's havin' some trouble hitting her notes."

Frank nodded. "Yeah, I noticed that, too. But otherwise I think you're right. Believe it or not, Brian's put together a pretty good band."

Rap . . . rap . . . Someone was knocking on their door.

"Ellie, Frankie," Toni said in a low voice. "Open up!"

"Why?" Frank asked.

"'Cause it's me and Sabrina, that's why."

"Geez, now what?" Eddie whispered.

"Get your wig on," Frank hissed.

"Oh, man, I'm gettin' tired of this." Eddie groaned. He grabbed his wig and went into the bathroom. Frank went over to the door and opened it. Toni and Sabrina came in. Sabrina was carrying a small makeup case.

"Hey, what's up?" Frank asked in his girl voice.

"I came over to work on your hands," Sabrina said.

"And I came over to see if Ellie felt like checkin' out the neighborhood," Toni said, looking around the room. "Don't tell me she's in the bathroom again."

"Yeah." Frank nodded.

"Wow, that girl spends more time in the john than anyone I ever met," Toni said, shaking her head.

"Here I am." Eddie came out of the bathroom wearing the blond wig.

"Listen, cutie pie," Toni said, "there's a bar about half a mile down the road. You and me are gonna go check it out."

"Huh?" Eddie looked at Frank. "What about you, er, Frankie?"

"I'm gonna stay here with Sabrina," Frank said with a quick wink. "She wants to work on my hands. But you should definitely go."

"To a bar?" Eddie gasped.

"Sure," Toni said. "Who knows, there might even be some guys there."

"Guys?" Eddie looked stricken.

"Where'd you come from, a convent?" Toni asked.

"But Brian said it should be an early night," Eddie protested.

"If it was up to Brian, life would be real dull, honey," Toni said. "Now come on."

"She's right," said Frank, who couldn't wait to be alone with Sabrina. "You really should go, Ellie. You need to get out and meet some men."

Eddie gave him a look like he wanted to kill him. "Sure, Frankie, that's just what I need."

"Come on," Toni said, taking Eddie by the arm and leading him out. "Let's get out of here before Brian does a bed check."

Eddie and Toni headed for the door. Frank followed them.

"Have fun." He waved. "Don't do anything I wouldn't do."

FRANK CLOSED THE DOOR AND turned back to Sabrina. "That Toni's wild, isn't she?"

"I think it's good," Sabrina said. "She's got a lot of spunk."

Then she patted the bed beside her. "Come on, let's get to work."

Frank sat down on the bed and Sabrina opened the makeup case.

"Now let me see those hands," Sabrina said. She took one of Frank's hands and held it in her own. "Wow, it doesn't look like you've ever done anything with them."

"I always thought it was a hopeless cause," Frank said with a dejected sigh.

Sabrina pressed her thumb down into his palm. They were sitting side by side, their thighs touching, their faces only a foot apart. Frank could smell the scent of her hair.

"And your hands are so tense," Sabrina

said, kneading his palm with her thumb and fingers.

"I've been playing guitar all day," said Frank.

Sabrina put his hand down and stood up. "Come with me, Frankie. We're going to soak them."

They went into the bathroom and Sabrina ran hot water into the sink. Then she got a chair for Frank to sit in while he soaked his hands. She sat down on the toilet cover beside him.

"Doesn't that feel good?" Sabrina asked while Frankie soaked his hands.

"Yeah."

"You really have to take better care of your hands, Frankie," Sabrina said. "Guys care about things like that."

Frank looked down at Sabrina's hands. They were long and slender.

"You have beautiful hands," he said in his girl voice.

"Thanks." Sabrina blushed a little.

Frank lifted his hands out of the water and ran the tips of his fingers over Sabrina's hands. He gazed into her eyes. "Everything about you is beautiful," he said.

For a moment, Sabrina just gazed back at him. Then she seemed to snap out of it.

"Let's get those hands back where they belong," she said with a self-conscious chuckle. She made Frank put his hands back in the sink.

After a while, Sabrina told him to take his hands out of the water. She dried them with a towel and then put some kind of lotion on them and started to massage them, squeezing his palms and fingers gently. Suddenly she paused and stared at his knuckles.

"What's wrong?" Frank asked.

"What are all these scars?" she asked.

Frank looked down. His knuckles were covered with scars from fights. "Oh, uh, my cats," he said quickly. "I used to have cats. They were a little rough sometimes."

"I'll say." Sabrina started to massage his hands again. "Does it feel good?" she asked softly.

"Oh, yes," Frank said. They were facing each other now, looking into each other's eyes. Sabrina was the most beautiful, the most delicate and soft female he'd ever laid eyes on. She was like a dream. Frank wanted to pinch himself to make sure she was really real.

"Okay," Sabrina said. "You hands feel a lot less tense now. Come on, I want to work on those cuticles."

Sabrina started to push his cuticles back and clip them with a tiny scissors.

"Does your boyfriend ever admire your hands?" Frank asked.

"Who? Joe?" Sabrina shook her head. "He doesn't notice anything."

"That's too bad," Frank said.

Sabrina nodded. "To tell you the truth, Frankie, I'm sort of hoping he gets too involved back home and sort of forgets about me."

"Why?" Frank asked.

"Well, he isn't really my type," Sabrina said.

Frank was delighted to hear that. But it did raise some questions in his mind. "If he isn't your type, then how come you're with him?"

"Oh, well, at first he was really nice," Sabrina said. "He took me to the city and to all kinds of expensive places I'd never been to before. He had so much money. I'd never gone out with anyone like that. It was fun."

"Where's he get all that money?" Frank asked.

"Well, that's part of the problem," Sabrina said. "I'm really not supposed to tell you, but you can guess."

Frank nodded. "And that's what made it stop being fun?"

"That and he also started to get moody," Sabrina said with a shrug. "We stopped going to fun places, and if I said I wanted to go out he'd get so mad he'd scare me. I sort of wanted to break up, but I was afraid."

"That he'd hurt you?"

Sabrina sort of shrugged and nodded. "I don't know what he'd do. I just know he carries a knife and he's not afraid to use it. And then he helped me get this job, and . . . I don't know. I'm not sure what I should do now."

"Well, if you really don't like him, maybe you should break up," Frank said.

"I know," Sabrina said as she filed Frank's nails. "But I'm still scared. I mean, I don't know if he'd really hurt me or not, but I really like being a singer, and I'm afraid if we broke up, Joe might make Brian fire me just for spite. One thing about Joe is that he gets insanely jealous. I mean, if a guy so much as *looks* at me he'll go crazy."

"Don't I know it," Frank said.

Sabrina scowled. "You do?"

"Well, I mean, I know the *type*," Frank quickly said.

Sabrina nodded. "To tell you the truth, Frankie, I really don't know what to do."

"Sometimes it's really hard to know," Frank said sympathetically.

Sabrina fixed him with her large brown eyes. Frank gazed into them and almost felt dizzy from the emotions welling up inside him.

"What would you do?" Sabrina asked.

Frank realized she could be right about the singing job, but for a different reason. Sabrina wasn't that good. If Brian knew that he wasn't gonna get beaten up by Joe, he might decide to let her go.

"I'd . . . I'd keep my options open," he said. "Don't do anything drastic about Joe, but at the same time see what's out there."

"I think that's easier said than done," Sabrina said. "It looks like all we're going to do for the next few weeks is rehearse. And there's no way I'm sneaking out with Toni at night to go to bars."

"I know. It's not really your scene," Frank said. "Maybe you just have to be patient."

Sabrina finished filing his nails. "Okay, now it's time for a base coat." She took some jars of polish out of the box and started to paint Frank's nails. "So what color would you like?"

"Uh, how about clear?" Frank suggested,

hoping that the time might come soon when he could dress up like a guy again. If it did, he didn't want to have colorful fingernails.

"Oh, come on, Frankie," Sabrina said. "You have to let yourself have some fun."

"I have fun," Frank said in his girl voice.

"I mean, with your looks," Sabrina said.

Twenty minutes later, Frank had a set of bright red fingernails. He couldn't believe he'd agreed to it. But that was the effect Sabrina had on him. He would have done almost anything she said.

"So what do you think?" Sabrina asked.

Frank stared down at his bright red nails in utter disbelief. "They're, uh, great."

"Let's see what Brian says about your hands now," Sabrina said, giving him a wink and getting up. She started putting the nail stuff back in the makeup kit. Then she yawned. "I guess I better get back to my room."

"Yeah." Frank said. He hated to see her go.

"See you tomorrow," she said and went out the door.

Frank gave her a little wave, then looked down at his bright red nails again. This was too much! Just too much!

Rap! Rap! He had just gotten ready for bed when someone knocked on the door. Frank went to the door. "Who is it?"

"Ellie."

Frank pulled open the door and Eddie staggered in. His wig was crooked and his clothes were all twisted.

"What happened to you?" Frank asked.

"Man, can that girl drink!" Eddie stumbled over to his bed and flopped down on his back.

"Toni?"

Eddie nodded.

"I thought you went to meet guys," Frank said.

"Yeah, we did that too," Eddie groaned.

"What happened?"

"They got fresh," Eddie said.

"So what'd you do?"

"Beat 'em up," Eddie said.

"Toni, too?" Frank asked in disbelief.

Eddie nodded. "Oh, yeah, not only can she drink, she can fight too."

"I don't believe it," Frank said.

"Believe it," said Eddie. "And be a pal and get me some aspirin."

"Where is it?" Frank asked.

"In my makeup kit," Eddie said. Then he slapped his hand against his forehead. "Oh, man, I can't believe I just said that!"

Frank went into the bathroom and found the aspirin. He came back out and handed Eddie a few tablets and a glass of water. Eddie was staring at Frank's hands.

"What happened to you?"

"Sabrina did my nails," Frank said.

Eddie shook his head and took the aspirin. "This is really sick."

"You're starting to sound like your sister," Frank said.

"Well, maybe for once in her life she was right."

THE BAND PRACTICED DAY AND night. With Frank's encouragement, Eddie snuck out a lot at night and went drinking with Toni, while Frank stayed in the room with Sabrina and just talked or watched TV. Frank felt that they were becoming closer and closer. The problem was, Sabrina thought she was becoming close with another girl.

Then two nights before the band was scheduled to play their first real gig, Sabrina didn't come into the room.

"You seen Sabrina?" Frank asked Toni when she came to get Eddie to go out drinking.

"She went down to the office," Toni said. "There was a phone call for her." She turned to Eddie. "Ready to boogie, Ellie?"

"Sure thing," Eddie said with a groan.

After Toni and Eddie snuck out to go down to the bar, Frank checked his makeup and decided to stroll down to the office and get a soda. Sabrina was standing in the vestibule, talking on the pay phone. She didn't look happy, but when she saw Frank, she forced a smile onto her face and gave him a little wave.

Not wanting to make it look like he was waiting for her, Frank went into the motel office to get a can of pop. As he fed money into the soda machine, he caught a glimpse of his reflection. Uh-oh! He looked like he was out of alignment again! Frank reached under the loose sweatshirt he usually wore at night and started to adjust the cups.

Just then the door to the motel office and Brian came in. The manager stopped and scowled at Frank, who quickly removed his hands from under the sweatshirt. The two just stared at each other. Brian was frowning. Frank didn't know what to say, so he just nodded and went out with his pop. He passed the vestibule again. Sabrina was still on the phone. Frank signaled to her to ask if he should wait, and she nodded.

He walked a few feet out into the parking lot so it wouldn't look like he was listening in on her conversation. A thin layer of low clouds reflected the lights from the ground, and off in the distance he could see the glow of Beach City, where they would be playing their first gig. Nearly two weeks had passed and they hadn't even *seen* the beach yet. But all that would change soon.

Finally Sabrina hung up. She sighed and shook her head.

"What is it?" Frank asked in his girl voice as he stepped toward her.

"Joe," Sabrina said. They started walking back to the room. "He's coming down for our first gig."

"So he didn't forget you after all," Frank said, feeling immensely disappointed.

"No. He actually sounded sweet and nice again. He said he really missed me."

Frank winced slightly. "So what are you going to do?"

"See him, what else?" Sabrina said. "I mean, maybe he's changed. Maybe he realized how much he missed me and decided to be nice from now on."

"And what about the other thing?" Frank asked.

"Huh?" Sabrina didn't follow.

"How he makes his living."

"Oh, I guess I'll just have to see," Sabrina said.

"Well, I know you hope that he's changed," Frank warned her. "But I know that kind of guy. Sooner or later they're bound to get mean again. It's in the blood."

"You're probably right, Frankie," Sabrina said. "But I guess I have to give him a chance."

They got back to Sabrina's room and she stopped.

"Aren't you coming over?" Frank asked.

"Not tonight, Frankie." Sabrina seemed sad. "I think I want to be alone."

She pulled open the door to her room. Then she stopped and looked back at Frankie.

Without warning, she leaned toward him and gave him a kiss on the cheek.

"What was that for?" Frank asked, startled.

"You've been a really good friend these last two weeks," Sabrina said. "I don't know what I'd do without you."

If you only knew, Frank couldn't help thinking.

"See you tomorrow," Sabrina said and closed the door.

Frank continued down to his room. It was bad news that Sharkbait Joe was coming down for the gig. He felt like he'd made some progress with Sabrina over the past few weeks, but only as a girl. If he really wanted things to change between Sabrina and him, he was going to have to do something, and fast.

Later, he was lying in bed in the dark, trying to figure out what to do when the door opened and Eddie staggered in. As he did most nights, he pulled off his wig, unhooked his bra, and flopped down on the bed.

"I can't do this anymore," he groaned.

"Neither can I," said Frank.

Eddie stared at him. "I'm talkin' about goin' out drinkin' with Toni every night. What are *you* talking about?"

"Being Frankie with Sabrina," Frank said. "I gotta be a guy with her. And I gotta do it soon because Sharkbait Joe's coming down to see the band at our first gig the night after tomorrow."

"Well, I know what we gotta do," Eddie said. "We gotta get out of here and go back to

Clotsburg. I've had it with this girl stuff, band or no band."

"I can't go," Frank said.

"Yeah, yeah, because of Sabrina," Eddie said. "Well, I hate to say this, Frank, but how about I go and you stay?"

"The band's nowhere without a drummer," Frank said.

"That's life," Eddie said. "If I have to get dressed up in those girl's clothes and go out drinking one more night with Toni I'm gonna turn into—"

"A serial killer." Frank finished the sentence for him.

"How'd you know?" Eddie asked.

"Because that's what you *always* say, Eddie."

"This time I mean it," Eddie said.

"Look, Eddie, just give me one more week," Frank said. "That's all I ask."

"Good, 'cause that's all you're gonna get."

12

THE NEXT AFTERNOON, FRANK'S luck changed. Brian announced that since they were playing their first gig the next night, he was giving them this night off. Not only that, but he was going to take everyone over to Beach City for the evening.

Back in their room, Frank packed a shirt, shoes, and his makeup kit into a small bag. "This could be my lucky break, man."

"How's that?" Eddie asked as he pulled on the blond wig.

"Everyone's going into town," Frank said. "Well, Frankie's gonna disappear, and Frank's gonna appear and run into Sabrina again."

"Yeah, but somehow Frank's gotta turn back into Frankie before he comes back to the motel," Eddie said, leaning forward toward the mirror as he applied his lipstick.

"That's what they made bathrooms for," Frank said.

"Really?" Eddie pretended to act surprised. "I thought they had some other purpose altogether."

"Very funny." Frank smirked.

"Look, all kidding aside," Eddie said. "I really hope this works, because I can't take much more of this. I gotta get back to being Eddie again."

"You sure?" Frank joked. "I'm kind of getting used to you as a girl."

"Yeah, well that's part of the problem," Eddie said. "I'm kind of getting used to me as a girl too. If I don't get back to being a guy pretty soon, I'm worried I may forget."

They went out and got into the van with the girls. It was early evening now, and the summer sun was still high in the western sky. As usual, Frank sat with Sabrina and Eddie sat with Toni.

"I can't believe the slave driver is finally giving us a night off," Toni grumbled.

"Just goes to show he has a heart," Frank said.

Toni turned to Eddie. "Ready to party down, honey?"

"What else?" Eddie groaned, rolling his mascaraed eyes.

Frank felt Toni tap him on the shoulder. "What about you two?"

"I'm up for some fun," Sabrina said. She gave Frank a questioning look.

"Oh, uh, I have a very elderly aunt who lives in town," Frank said. "Now that we finally have a night off, I really have to go see her."

Sabrina looked disappointed.

"You sure know how to have fun, Frankie," Toni said behind them.

Sabrina gestured toward Ann, Rachel, and Chrissy, who were sitting together as usual in the front of the van. "Should we ask them?"

"The three nuns?" Toni smirked. "Sure, honey, if you want to sit on the beach and write poetry."

"Uh, not tonight," Sabrina said with a smile.

It wasn't long before they got to Beach City. The main street was lined with motels, music clubs, fast-food places, and surf shops. Brian parked the van in the parking lot of a small shopping mall across the street from the bus station.

"Okay, everyone, we meet back here at midnight, no later," he said. "If anyone needs me, I'll be over at the Surfside Club, checking it out for tomorrow night."

Just as Toni had predicted, "the three nuns" said they were going to go down to the beach. Meanwhile, Toni, Sabrina, and Eddie were ready to go barhopping.

"You sure you can't come, Frankie?" Sabrina asked.

"Well, tell me where you're going just in case my aunt goes to bed early," Frank said, as he set the alarm in his watch for ten minutes before midnight.

"That's easy," said Toni. "We're gonna start here and go that way." She pointed down the main drag.

"Great." Frank waved good-bye. "Maybe I'll catch you later."

"Have fun with your aunt." Eddie smiled and waved back.

Frank waited until they were out of sight. Then he looked around. Next to the shopping mall was a motel with rooms that opened onto a central courtyard. Several of the rooms were open while chamber maids cleaned them out. Frank picked up his bag and walked into the courtyard. He waited until no one was looking and then slipped into one of the open rooms.

He went into the bathroom and locked the door. Wow, a clean bathroom for once! What a change. He stared at himself in the mirror. Eddie was right. He was so used to seeing Frankie in the mirror that he'd almost forgotten what Frank looked like. He turned on the faucet and splashed water on his face, then scrubbed the makeup off. When he looked back into the mirror again, he was Frank. What a relief to be himself again!

He pulled his hair back into a ponytail and changed into Frank's clothes. Great, he was ready to go.

"Long time, no see, partner," he said, looking at his reflection in the mirror. Then he packed Frankie's clothes in the bag.

Rap . . . rap . . . "Someone in there?" a voice called.

Uh,oh. Frank pulled open the bathroom door. A chambermaid wearing a gray uniform, and carrying a mop stood outside.

"What're you doing in here?" she asked.

"I, uh, just really had to go to the bathroom," Frank said.

"Well, you know you're not supposed to be in here," she said.

"Yeah, I'm just going." Frank took off.

Back on the street, he started in the direction Toni said the girls would follow. But first he stopped at the bus station. Inside, next to a row of pay telephones, he found some lockers and left the bag with Frankie's clothes. Back on the street again, the first bar he came to was a run-down smokey place with a jukebox. Frank went in and stood at the bar.

"Help you?" A burly-looking bartender asked.

"I'm looking for three girls," Frank said. "One's a real knockout, one's a real sexy black chick, and the third's short with long curly blond hair."

"Ain't seen 'em," the bartender said. Then he stared down at Frank's hands and scowled.

Frank followed his eyes. Oh, crap! He was still wearing the bright red nail polish!

"Uh, see ya around." Frank quickly left the bar. Across the street was a drugstore. He went in and bought a bag of cotton balls and nail polish remover. Outside he sat on a bus stop bench and removed the red polish from his nails.

Now he was ready to find Sabrina.

He found them at a place called the Ocean Club. It had a tropical surfing motif, with a fake thatch roof over the bar and surfboards hanging from the walls. Loud music was playing and the crowd looked pretty young.

Sabrina, Toni, and Eddie were sitting at the bar, sipping frozen tropical drinks through straws. Pretending he didn't see them, Frank went up to the bar and sat down on a stool. He ordered a beer. Out of the corner of his eye he glanced up at the mirror behind the bar, hoping to catch Sabrina's eye.

He caught someone's eye all right. But it wasn't Sabrina. It was—Toni.

When their eyes met, hers widened slightly and a smile grew on her lips. Caught by surprise, Frank smiled back maybe a second longer than he should have. Then he looked back at his drink.

Toni started to whisper to Eddie and Sabrina. Frank felt their eyes on him. He looked over and his eyes met Sabrina's.

"It's you!" she gasped.

Toni frowned. "You know him?"

"Well, yes . . . I mean, not really." Sabrina seemed a little flustered.

"Just my luck," Toni muttered.

"What are you doing here?" Sabrina asked. She and Toni moved a little closer to him.

"Just decided to come down to the beach for a while," Frank replied. "How about you?"

"Well, we're in this band," Sabrina said. "This is Toni and Ellie. They're in the band with me."

Toni gave him a little wave. Eddie held out his hand and winked coyly. "Hiya handsome."

Frank ignored him and looked at Sabrina. "So where's your band playing?"

"Well, tomorrow night's our first gig," Sabrina said. "We'll be playing at the Surfside Club."

"Maybe you could come see us," Eddie said.

Frank narrowed his eyes at Eddie, then turned to Sabrina. "Well, uh, gee, I'd love to, but I think I'm busy tomorrow night."

"Oh." Sabrina looked a little disappointed.

"But I'll come see you another time," Frank quickly added.

Sabrina brightened.

An awkward moment followed. Frank wanted to spend some time with Sabrina. The problem was Toni and Eddie.

"It's funny how we're always meeting each other in these weird situations," Frank said.

"Weird?" Toni scowled.

"With lots of people around." As Frank said this he kicked Eddie's leg lightly trying to make sure his buddy got the hint. But Eddie either didn't notice or didn't want to notice.

"Oh, tell us where you two have met before," Eddie said in his girl voice.

"Back in Clotsburg," Frank replied tersely.

"Why didn't you have time to talk then?" Eddie asked.

"Because there were other people around." This time Frank gave Eddie a harder kick.

"Ow!" Eddie cried.

"What happened?" Sabrina asked.

"Uh, nothing," Eddie said, glaring at Frank. "You know what, Toni? I get the feeling these two would like to be alone. Why don't we move on to the next place? These guys can catch up with us later."

"Oh, okay," Toni said. She tapped Sabrina on the shoulder. "Be good now, you hear?"

Sabrina nodded and grinned. Eddie and Toni left the club.

Frank turned back to Sabrina and smiled. Finally, they were alone.

13

THEY STAYED AT THE OCEAN CLUB and talked for a while. But when the bartender started hinting that they ought to buy another round of drinks, Frank asked if she'd like to go see the beach. Sabrina said she'd like that. She hadn't seen the beach yet.

The sun had gone down while they were in the bar. The beach was dark except for a few couples and groups of people sitting here and there on the sand, talking or listening to music. The sky was filling with stars. A steady rumble filled the air as the waves rolled in and crashed on the sand. Frank and Sabrina took off their shoes and rolled up their pants and walked barefoot at the surf's edge.

"Like the ocean?" Frank asked.

"Yes," Sabrina answered.

"I wouldn't mind living down here all the time," Frank said. "I know it gets pretty cold and desolate in the winter, but that would be okay too."

"It would be nice to be here alone, when everyone else is gone," Sabrina said.

Frank glanced at her. "Why do I get the feeling you don't get to have much time alone?"

"Because I don't."

"Maybe you'd be happier if I left you alone right now?" Frank said.

"Oh, no," Sabrina said. "It's nice here with you. It's just other times I wish I could be left alone a little more."

"Like when?" Frank asked.

"Just other times," Sabrina said, obviously not willing to talk about Sharkbait Joe with him.

Frank pointed up at the sky. "They say somewhere out there must be another planet with life on it. You believe that?"

Sabrina looked up and nodded. "I think so."

"You think maybe out there is a planet and there's a beach and on that beach are these two people, and well, it's kind of complicated, but there's something that sort of draws them together?"

They were standing side by side. Sabrina glanced at him for a second, then looked back at the sky and nodded slowly. "Yes, I think that's possible."

"And it's kind of weird because these two people don't know each other very well," Frank said. "They hardly ever get to see each other. But they think about each other a lot. Somehow they have this feeling . . . "

"But it's complicated because there are other people involved," Sabrina said.

"They both wish it wasn't so complicated,"

Frank said, turning to face her. Sabrina turned to face him. He looked into her eyes. In the dark they were deep and endless. Their faces were maybe a foot apart. Frank felt himself drawn to her. Like it was magnetism. He moved closer. Sabrina looked up at him. It was hard to know what she was thinking, but Frank decided to take a chance. Who knew if he'd ever get another opportunity? It might be now or never . . .

"Whoops!" someone shouted.

Frank and Sabrina spun around.

Someone short and stocky with long curly blond hair was running across the beach toward them, waving her arms. It was Eddie!

"Oh, uh, sorry to interrupt," he gasped in his girl voice when he reached them.

"That's okay," Sabrina said. "Is something wrong, Ellie?"

"Well, uh, I just happened to be walking down Main Street and guess who drove by in a black Jeep?" Eddie said.

Sabrina looked shocked. "He's here?"

Eddie nodded and glanced at Frank. "With that big friend of his. They're stopping outside every club and looking in. I have a feeling they're looking for someone."

Sabrina sighed and shook her head. Then she looked at Frank. "I better go back. Otherwise he's going to wonder where I've been."

Now Toni came across the beach. "So, I see you found them," she said to Eddie. She turned to Frank and Sabrina. "Boy, I've never seen anything like this girl. One second we're bopping along the street, then she sees something and boom! She takes off like she's seen a ghost."

"Well, thanks, Ellie." Sabrina started up the beach.

"Hey, Sabrina," Frank said. "Don't forget those two people on that other planet."

"I won't," Sabrina said.

They watched her walk away into the dark.

"Two people on another planet?" Toni scowled at Frank. "What have *you* been drinking?"

"I'll tell you next time I see you," Frank said. "Right now I better get going."

"Hey, wait a minute, handsome." Toni slid her arm through his. "What's the rush? Just because Miss Gorgeous is gone doesn't mean the party has to end."

But Frank knew the sooner he got back into his Frankie disguise the better. "Believe me," he said, gently taking her arm out of his, "if it was any other night it would be a different story."

Toni looked disappointed. "Party pooper."

"Yeah," said Eddie. "Party pooper."

Frank just waved at them and headed up the beach toward the strip. There were crowds of people walking around, barhopping, window shopping, and just enjoying the evening. Cars cruised up and down slowly, filled with guys checking out girls or girls checking out guys. Frank walked down the sidewalk toward the bus station.

Then he stopped. The black Jeep was parked outside the bus station, and Grungy Arnie was sitting in the passenger seat! Frank looked at his watch. It was 11:45. He had fifteen minutes to turn back into Frankie and meet the van.

Frank looked around. There had to be another entrance to the bus station. He went down an alley around to the back. Just as he'd hoped, there was a back entrance. Frank went in. The bus station was filled with kids carrying backpacks and suitcases, all coming from and going to the beach. Frank went to the coin locker, slid the key in, and took out his bag of Frankie clothes.

All he had to do was change clothes and everything would be fine, he thought as he shut the locker door. He turned around and suddenly froze. Sharkbait Joe was standing at a pay phone ten feet away. Frank felt the blood drain out of his face. Sharkbait glanced at him, then looked away, then did a double take. He squinted, as if he couldn't place Frank for a moment. Then he figured it out.

"You!" Sharkbait took a step toward Frank, but he forgot he was holding the phone. The cord went tight and . . . *Clunk!* The receiver slipped out of his hands.

"Crap!" Sharkbait turned and grabbed the phone.

Frank took off, running through the bus station and out the front doors.

"Hey!" someone shouted.

Frank stopped and turned. Grungy Arnie was climbing out of the Jeep.

"We wanna talk to you!" Arnie shouted.

Talk? That was a good one. Frank took off down the sidewalk and ducked into the first bar he came to. It was a small, scuzzy place with a couple of old guys hunched over at the bar, sipping drinks and staring at a baseball game on the TV. They gave Frank a look as he hurried past them and into the bathroom in back.

"Hey!" shouted the burly bartender. "That bathroom's for patrons only!"

"Gimme a beer!" Frank shouted and slammed the bathroom door behind him.

The bathroom was small, cramped, and smelled—like a bathroom. Frank stripped off his shirt and boots and quickly put on his padded bra and Frankie clothes. He pulled his hair out of the ponytail and brushed it out over his shoulders. Then he did a quick makeup job. The alarm on his watch beeped. Jeez, it was midnight!

Frank pushed open the bathroom door, took two steps—and stopped dead.

Sharkbait Joe and Grungy Arnie were standing at the bar, talking to the bartender!

They all turned and looked at Frank. A fresh glass of beer stood on the bar. The bartender frowned. Frank took a deep breath, marched up to the bar and chugged half the glass. He reached into his pocket, pulled out a couple of rumpled dollar bills, and put them on the bar. The bartender just stared at him.

Sharkbait Joe and Arnie turned back to the bartender.

"We're lookin' for a guy," Joe said. "About six foot tall. Brown ponytail."

The bartender looked at Frank again. Frank reached into his pocket and fished out a five-dollar bill and laid it on the bar. The bartender looked at the money and then turned back to Sharkbait Joe and Arnie.

"Ain't seen him," he said.

Joe and Arnie left the bar. Frank felt himself go limp with relief. He finished his beer and put the empty glass down on the bar.

"Thanks," he said in his male voice as he got up to leave.

The bartender just kept staring at him.

Back on the street, he hurried toward the shopping mall parking lot. Brian was standing beside the van with his hands on his hips, looking impatient.

"I said midnight, Frankie," he said as Frank hurried up and climbed onto the van.

"Sorry," Frank said in his girl voice.

Inside the van, he sat down next to Sabrina. He was breathing hard and deeply. Someone tapped him on the shoulder. Frank turned around to find Eddie.

"How was Great Aunt Tilly?" Eddie asked in his girl voice.

"Oh, just fine," Frank replied in *his* girl voice.

"So what did you two spend the evening talking about?" Eddie asked.

"Oh, just about everything," Frank said. "And how about you? How was your night?"

"Well, Sabrina met someone," Eddie said.

Frank glanced at Sabrina. "Oh, do tell."

"It was nothing," Sabrina said.

"Nothing?" Frank felt a little disappointed.

"Go on," said Toni. "He was a hunk. You guys must've been together for a couple of hours."

Sabrina shrugged.

Then I saw her boyfriend Joe in town," Eddie said. "You know, the one with the Jeep."

"Oh, really?" Frank, now Frankie, pretended not to know anything about that.

"Sometimes I wish there were only girls in the world," Sabrina said with a sigh.

"Oh, you don't mean that," Eddie said. "That wouldn't be any fun at all."

"Maybe not," said Sabrina. "But it sure would be a lot easier."

Brian started to drive the van back to the motel. Frank waited to see if Sabrina would say anything more about meeting him, but she didn't. The ride back to the motel was a quiet one. When they got there, Brian told everyone to sleep late the next morning.

"I want everyone well rested for tomorrow night," he said. "Remember, we either knock 'em dead or it's back to Clotsburg."

Frank and Eddie went into their room. Frank slid the chain on the door. Eddie pulled off his wig and sat down on the corner of the bed to pull off his shoes.

"Okay," he said. "You finally got to spend some time with Sabrina as Frank. That means it's time to skate, Frank."

"No." Frank went into the bathroom to wash the makeup off.

"What do you mean, no?" Eddie asked. "This ain't workin'. You heard what Sabrina said. She saw you tonight and it was nothing. She wishes all guys would just disappear."

"I know that's what she said to *you*," Frank said. "But it's not what she said to me."

"Right," Eddie said. "To you she talked about those people on that other planet."

Frank came out of the bathroom, drying his face on a towel. "Look, Eddie, you said you wanted to have one last good summer before your parents made you get a job. You wanted to be in a band at the beach. This is everything you wanted."

"Except I have to wear a wig, a dress, and falsies all the time," Eddie muttered.

Frank grinned. "Hey, nothing's perfect."

EVERYONE SLEPT LATE THE NEXT day. Then Brian took them over to the storage locker for a light rehearsal. When the rehearsal was over, he backed the van up to the locker.

"Okay, girls, time to pack up the equipment and take it over to the Surfside Club," he said.

Everyone groaned. Moving guitars wasn't a big deal, but moving the drums and amps and sound system was. It took hours to load. Then they all got in the van and went into town and parked behind the Surfside Club. They moved all their equipment in through the back of the club and set it up on stage.

"I can't believe they expect us girls to do this," Eddie complained as he lugged his bass drum in.

"Yeah," said Rachel, the keyboard player. "We should have roadies."

"Hey," Brian said, "you should feel lucky just to have a place to play."

Once all the equipment was set up, they gathered in the small dressing room backstage and waited until it was time to go on. The dressing room was hardly larger than a walk-in closet. The only furniture was a tattered old couch and some rickety wooden chairs.

"Gee, this is even worse than the storage locker," Ann said.

Sabrina sat on the couch, rubbing her hands and fidgeting. Frank, as Frankie, sat down next to her.

"Nervous?" he asked.

"Sure," she said. "Aren't you?"

Frank shrugged. Actually, he was nervous, but he knew from experience that he shouldn't show it. Not that he was trying to be macho, but acting nervous would just make everyone else worse.

"Let me give you a massage," he said, getting up.

"A massage?" Sabrina scowled.

"Sure," Frank said. "You gave me one the other day. Now it's my turn." He stood behind her, gathered her long thick hair in his hands, and swept it away from her neck. Then he began to massage her shoulders. The muscles felt hard as rocks.

"Wow, you are tense," he said.

"Hmmmm." Sabrina closed her eyes. She relaxed a little and smiled. "That's nice."

Frank kept working her shoulder muscles. Gradually they grew more pliant. Her skin was smooth and soft. He slowly worked his fingers up the back of her neck and back down over her shoulders to the tops of her arms.

"Gee, I wonder who's enjoying that more?" Eddie, dressed as Ellie, asked, coming over. "Do me next, Frankie?"

Frank gave him a cold look.

"Yeah, just as I thought," Eddie sniffed. "Story of my life."

"What is?" Sabrina asked, opening her eyes.

"The pretty girls get all the attention." Eddie pouted.

"Hey, come over here and sit." Sabrina pointed to the floor in front of the couch. Eddie went over and sat down on the floor. Sabrina started to massage his shoulders while Frank massaged hers.

"Now *this* is the life!" Eddie said with a sigh.

Suddenly the door to the dressing room swung open and Sharkbait Joe came in. Frank stopped breathing.

"Hey, Sabrina." Joe started toward the couch.

Brian stepped into his path. "I'm sorry, no visitors before the show. You have to leave."

"What are you talkin' about?" Joe glowered at him. "You remember what happened last time?"

Brian glanced back at Sabrina. "Actually, I forget. Perhaps you'd like to refresh my memory."

Frank knew Joe wouldn't say or do anything in front of Sabrina. Joe narrowed his eyes at Brian, but turned and left. As soon as the door closed, everyone clapped.

"Nice going, Brian!" Toni yelled.

Brian grinned and bowed. "Now get ready, everyone. This is serious."

• • •

The band played really well that night. More importantly, the crowd really loved them and the music. They did two encores and left the stage with the audience still shouting for more. Even the three nuns were excited.

"That was great!" Chrissy cried when they got back to the dressing room.

Everyone went around slapping high fives and hugging each other. But they were worried too. Brian was outside, talking to the club's owner. The night didn't mean anything unless the owner wanted them to come back and do it again the next night.

The dressing room door opened and Brian came in. He looked serious. Frank noticed he had his hands behind his back.

"What'd he say?" Rachel asked.

"Yeah," said Chrissy, "does he want us?"

"He said . . . " A big grin broke out on Brian's face. "He loved you! He wants you for two weeks!"

The girls screamed and started hugging each other again. Brian pulled two bottles of champagne out from behind his back, and they shared a bunch of toasts. Then people started banging on the dressing door, wanting the band to come out.

"Go ahead," Brian said. "Just remember we gotta get back to the motel later and sleep. I want everyone rested up for tomorrow night."

Everyone left the dressing room and went out into the club. It was late now, and since the show was over, most of the patrons had left. The only people still hanging around were friends of Brian, Toni, and the three nuns. And Sharkbait Joe.

Sharkbait and Sabrina sat at a table. Eddie and Frank, still dressed as Ellie and Frankie, sat down at the bar and ordered a couple of beers.

"Seein' them together must really kill you," Eddie said in a low voice.

"Yeah." Frank nodded and sipped his beer.

"You were right about one thing," Eddie said.

"What's that?" Frank asked.

"After that show tonight, I don't care so much about dressing up like a girl. It was great playin' in front of a live crowd again. Wearin' the clothes is just like puttin' on a costume. Remember those crazy outfits those guys from KISS used to wear?"

"Yeah."

"It's just part of the gig," Eddie said.

"So you're gonna stick with it?"

"Sure, why not?" Eddie said.

Frank smiled and patted him on the shoulder.

"Chill, Frank," Eddie whispered. "I don't think girls pat each other on the shoulder."

He was probably right. Frank glanced over at Sabrina and Joe, expecting to find their heads bowed close to each other, lost in a little world of their own. Instead, Joe was looking right back at him.

Frank quickly turned away and hunched over his beer.

"What is it?" Eddie asked.

"Looks like Sharkbait finds us interesting," Frank said in a low voice.

"Uh-oh." Eddie glanced over his shoulder, then looked back down at his beer. "Yeah, he's staring right at us. You don't think he's figured it out, do you?"

"If he has, he's a lot smarter than we think," Frank whispered.

"Crap," Eddie groaned. "Listen, whatever you do, don't look back at him again. We can't make it look like we think he knows something."

They sat there for a few moments, but afraid to turn around.

"This is ridiculous," Frank whispered. "Let's get out of here."

"Where're we gonna go?" Eddie whispered back.

"I don't care," Frank whispered. "Outside, in the van, anyplace but here."

"Okay, if you insist." Eddie picked up his glass and finished off his beer. Then he slid off the barstool and headed for the door.

"Hey, just a second." Across the room Sharkbait Joe stood up. He motioned Sabrina to stay seated. Then he started toward Frank and Eddie.

Eddie gave Frank a terrified look. This was it! They were dead meat.

AS SHARKBAIT JOE WALKED ACROSS the bar toward them, Frank wondered if they should run. No, they were probably safer there in the bar with Brian and everyone than they were alone out on the street with Joe.

Sharkbait stopped in front of them. He glanced at Frank and then turned his attention to Eddie. "Think I could talk to you outside for a second?"

Eddie's eyes darted toward Frank. "What about him? I mean, her?"

"I just wanna talk to you," Sharkbait said. "It's no big deal."

"Well, I don't know," Eddie stammered. "My mother told me never to go anywhere with strange men."

"Who you callin' strange?" Joe glowered at him.

"Uh, no one," Eddie said, stammering.

"Then, come on." Sharkbait smiled, revealing his broken teeth. "I ain't gonna hurt you."

The next thing Frank knew, Sharkbait and Eddie went out the door. Frank was tempted to follow, just to make sure his friend didn't come to any harm. But Sharkbait had left Sabrina sitting alone. It was an opportunity Frank couldn't resist. He sat down next to her.

"Hi, Frankie," Sabrina said with a weak smile.

"Hey, what's that all about?" he asked in his girl voice.

"Who knows?" Sabrina shrugged.

"Does he always just get up and leave you to go talk to other girls?" Frank asked.

"He does whatever he likes," she said.

"You don't sound very happy," Frank said.

"I owe him a lot," she said. "He got me into this band."

"But he hasn't changed?"

Sabrina shook her head.

"So you're just going to stay with him forever?" Frank asked. "Just because he did you one favor?"

Sabrina glared at him. She actually looked angry. Then she muttered, "I'd like to see *you* try and break up with him."

Frank realized he'd gone a little too far. "I'm sorry. It's none of my business."

Sabrina smiled weakly. "That's okay. I shouldn't have snapped. It's just kind of frustrating." Then she leaned toward him and spoke in a whisper. "Can I tell you a secret?"

"Okay," Frank whispered back.

"Remember last night Toni and Eddie said I ran into someone I knew?"

"Uh-huh."

"Well, I . . . I don't know him very well, but I sort of like him," Sabrina whispered. "I think he's staying somewhere in town. I just wish there was some way I could see him again."

That was just what Frank wanted to hear. "Maybe you can," he said.

"Are you kidding?" Sabrina asked. "Now that we're playing here every night, we'll never have any time. Not only will we have to play every night, but Brian wants to keep us rehearsing new songs so the crowd doesn't get tired of hearing the same old songs night after night."

"Then maybe you just have to be patient," Frank said.

"I guess," Sabrina said with a sigh. "One thing about guys. There always seems to be a never-ending supply."

That was not what Frank wanted to hear. "On the other hand, I'm sure the one you saw last night was someone special."

Sabrina nodded. "He did seem nice. But you never know. Joe was pretty nice when I first met him too."

Just then the door to the bar opened, and Eddie and Joe came back in. They came over to the table where Sabrina and Frank were sitting. Eddie looked sort of pale.

"Oh, well." Joe yawned. "It's gettin' kind of late. I'll come back and see your show tomorrow night." Then he bent forward, kissed Sabrina on the forehead, and left.

As soon as Joe was out the door, Frank turned to Eddie. "What was that all about?"

"Uh, nothing." Eddie glanced nervously at Sabrina and shook his head.

"Well, it had to be about something," Frank said.

"Believe me, Frankie, it was nothing," Eddie said in his girl voice. "He just wanted to know how I learned to play the drums so well."

Sabrina nodded. "Joe has a drum set at home. I think he wishes he could play them. I heard him play once and he wasn't very good."

Before they could talk anymore, Brian got up and slapped his hands together. "Okay, everyone, time to get back to the motel."

They went out to the van and drove back to the motel. Eddie was quiet during the trip home. It wasn't until Frank and Eddie were inside their room that they got to speak in private again.

"How come I don't believe that Sharkbait Joe just wanted to know about playin' the drums?" Frank asked as he unhooked his padded bra.

"You're right." Eddie slid open a drawer with his clothes in it and started to pull them all out.

"What are you doing?" Frank asked.

"Packing."

"Why?"

"I'm splitting," Eddie said.

"Why?"

"Why?" Eddie repeated. "Because Sharkbait Joe has a thing for me, that's why."

"He has a what?" Frank was certain he hadn't heard him right.

"A thing for me," Eddie said. "Like the hots,

you know? Like a boy/girl thing except what he don't know is the girl ain't what he thinks she is."

"You're telling me that Joe wants to drop Sabrina for you?" Frank asked in disbelief.

"He didn't tell me what he plans to do with Sabrina," Eddie said.

"Then what did he say?" Frank asked.

"You really wanna know?" Eddie asked.

"Yeah, sure."

"He told me he's always had a thing for girl drummers," Eddie said. "And he's always had a thing for long curly blonds. So all of a sudden I'm everything he ever wanted."

"Get real," Frank said.

"Hey, to quote him exactly, he said, 'Baby, you really make my bell ring.'"

"He said *that?*" Frank asked in disbelief.

"He sure did," said Eddie.

"What's he gonna do next?" Frank asked.

"I don't know," Eddie replied. "All I know is I ain't hanging around to find out."

"Wait," Frank said.

"What?"

"You can't leave now."

Eddie stared at Frank and shook his head. "Forget it, Frank. I don't care whether this fits into your plans for Sabrina or not. I don't care whether the band's got a great future or not. I don't care about nothing except gettin' outta here before Sharkbait Joe decides to give me a great big kiss."

"But don't you see that's not gonna happen?" Frank asked. "The only times he's gonna see you are when Sabrina is around. He's not gonna be able to do *anything*."

"That's what *you* say," Eddie said and started packing again.

"Eddie, you have to stay," Frank said.

"No way," Eddie said. "Not a chance. Give me one good reason."

"Because I'm beggin' you to," Frank said.

"What?" Eddie stared at him like he'd lost his mind.

"You heard me, Eddie," Frank said. "You gotta hang in. For the sake of the band, and Brian and Sabrina and me and you. You heard us tonight, man. This band's gonna go big time. And when it does, Sharkbait Joe's just gonna be a bad memory."

"No, Frank," Eddie said. "*You're* the one with the bad memory. Because you don't remember that you made Sharkbait look bad and then banged up his Jeep. It seems like you don't remember that Sharkbait wants to kill you."

"But he doesn't know it's us," Frank argued.

"Not right now, he don't. Tomorrow could be different."

"Not if we're smart," Frank said. "Right now he must think you're enough of a girl to have the hots for you."

Eddie just stared at him uncertainly.

"Remember, Eddie, this is your last chance," Frank reminded him. "Starting next summer it's a job for the rest of your life."

"But at least I'll be alive," Eddie said.

"Eddie . . . come on, do it for me, okay?"

Frank said. "If Joe drops Sabrina for you, I'll have my chance."

Eddie looked at him like he was crazy. "If Joe drops Sabrina for *me?* Are you psycho or what? I don't want anything to do with that creep."

"All you have to do is lead him on for a while," Frank said.

"Lead him on?" Eddie gasped. "You've really lost it, Frank. What if he wants to, you know . . . *do* stuff?"

"Just tell him you're not that kind of girl," Frank replied simply.

Eddie just stared at him in disbelief. "Okay, okay!" he yelled. "But I swear, if Joe kills me, I'll *kill* you!"

16

FOR THE NEXT WEEK, SHARKBAIT Joe came to the club every night. He smiled at Sabrina and sat with her between sets, but any time she wasn't around, he immediately turned his attention to Eddie. He winked, made suggestive remarks, and basically let Eddie know that if it wasn't for Sabrina, things between them would be a lot different.

One night, the band finished playing and went out into the club to relax before going home. But Eddie stayed behind in the dressing room.

"Aren't you gonna have a drink?" Frank asked as he put his guitar back in its case.

Eddie shook his head. The blond curls of his wig swept back and forth over his shoulders.

"Why not?" Frank asked.

"He's out there," Eddie said.

"Who? Joe?"

Eddie nodded.

"So?"

"Remember tonight during the intermission?" Eddie asked.

"Yeah?"

"He rubbed up against me as we went off the stage," Eddie said. "He was trying to feel me up. It's gone too far."

"Sabrina's out there," Frank said. "He won't do anything if she's around."

"Oh, no?" Eddie said. "Every time she looks away he gives me the eye. If we walk anywhere he puts his hand on my butt. I'm telling you, Frank, the guy's an animal."

"Look, just stick close to me and Sabrina tonight," Frank said. "He'll leave you alone."

They went out into the nightclub. It was late as usual and most of the patrons were gone. Joe, Arnie, and Sabrina were sitting at a table. Joe waved when he saw Frank and Eddie.

"Here we go again," Eddie muttered under his breath. They went over and sat down.

"Man, you girls are some players," Joe said. He patted Eddie on the hand. "I can't get over how hard you hit those skins, Ellie. You're like a one-girl show up there."

Frank glanced at Sabrina and she gave him a brittle smile. It was clear that she was aware that Joe was paying a lot of attention to Eddie.

"Thanks, Joe," Eddie replied in a sweet voice and gave him a smile while he gently withdrew his hand.

"Lemme ask you girls somethin'," Grungy Arnie said. "You said you was from Clotsburg?"

"That's right," Frank said.

"I'm from Clotsburg," Arnie said. "How come I ain't never seen either of you two around up there?"

"Oh, I guess we've always just kept to ourselves," Frank answered.

"You know Sal's Pizza?" Arnie asked.

Frank gave Eddie a nervous glance. It was impossible to live in Clotsburg and *not* know Sal's Pizza. It was the best pizza place around and a major hangout.

"Oh, of course we do," Frank said.

"That's good," Arnie said with a slow nod. "Sal's a good friend of mine. He knows everyone who comes into his joint. So I guess that means he'll remember you two musician chicks."

Frank and Eddie shared a nervous look. Then Eddie got up.

"Hey, where're you going?" Joe asked.

"I, uh . . . have to use the bathroom," Eddie stammered in his girl's voice.

"I'll go with you," Sabrina said and got up.

"Oh, no, that's not really necessary," Eddie said.

"Hey, it's okay," said Joe. "Chicks always go to the bathroom together. It's like a chick thing."

"A chick thing," Eddie repeated with a smile. "My, Joe, you have such a way with words."

Eddie and Sabrina left. As soon as they were out of sight, Joe turned to Frank.

"So, Frankie," he said. "What do you think of Sabrina?"

Frank's heart skipped a beat. What did Joe mean by that? Did he suspect something?

"I, uh, think she's a really sweet girl," Frank replied carefully in his girl voice.

"Yeah, sweet," Joe said. "But that Ellie, she's one hot babe, huh?"

"I guess," Frank said, wondering what Joe was getting at.

"Sabrina tells me that you and her have gotten to be pretty tight," Joe said.

Frank glanced at Arnie, trying to read his face. He just couldn't tell if they'd figured it out or not.

"I guess," Frank said.

"Hey, don't get me wrong," Joe said. "I think it's a good thing that she has a friend in the band. You know, someone with a shoulder she can lean on when things get tough."

"Why should things get tough?" Frank asked innocently.

"I'm just sayin' it's good for her to have a friend," Joe said. "Now tell me about Ellie."

"What about her?" Frank asked.

"She got a boyfriend?"

"Well, uh . . . " Frank wasn't sure how to answer.

"Hey, it don't matter, right?" Joe said. "I mean, I ain't seen anyone around, have you?"

Frank shook his head. Joe leaned back in his chair and smiled. He nudged Arnie with his elbow. "You know what they say—if you can't be with the one you love, better love the one you're with, right?"

Arnie nodded, but didn't crack a smile.

• • •

A little while later Brian came by and said it was time to get in the van and go back to the motel. Sabrina said good-bye to Joe. Everyone was quiet on the way home. It had been a long hard week and they were all exhausted.

Back in their motel room, Eddie flopped down on the bed, too tired to bother pulling his wig off.

"This is the end, dude," he said. "I don't know what tires me out more. Playin' the drums or dealing with that jerk. But it's too much."

"What was that thing with the bathroom tonight?" Frank asked from the bathroom where he was washing off his makeup.

"Don't you get it?" Eddie asked. "Arnie knows something's up."

"How come Arnie does and Joe doesn't?" Frank asked.

Eddie made a face. "Because Joe's *in love*, dummy. Love is blind, remember? He's lost in a love fog. Anyway, I can't hack it anymore. It's just not worth it."

Rap! Rap! There was a knock on the door. Frank stuck his head out of the bathroom.

"Who's that?" he whispered.

"Frank, you stupid?" Eddie whispered back. "It's Toni. She wants to go out drinkin' again. I swear, that girl never gets tired." He turned toward the door and said, "Not tonight, Toni."

"It's not Toni," a voice said.

Eddie and Frank gave each other startled looks.

"It's Brian," Frank whispered and pulled the bathroom door closed.

"Uh, just a minute," Eddie called in his girl voice. He jumped up and checked himself in the mirror, then went to the door and opened it. "Oh, Brian, what a surprise."

Frank kept the bathroom door open a hair and watched.

"Why'd you think it was Toni?" Brian asked.

"Uh, er, sometimes she comes over to borrow my hair dryer," Eddie said.

"In the middle of the night?" Brian frowned.

"Well, uh, yeah, if that's when she decides to wash her hair," Eddie said.

Brian looked around. "So where's Frankie?"

"I'm in here," Frank called from the bathroom in his girl voice.

"Can you come out for a minute?" Brian asked.

"Uh, not right now," Frank answered.

"If you're not decent, I'll get you a robe," Brian said.

"Oh, it's not that," Frank answered. He'd already washed off his makeup.

"Then what is it?" Brian asked.

"It's just a girl thing," Frank replied. "So how can we help you?"

"Well, I've got great news," Brian said. "I got back to my room tonight and there was a message from Sam."

"Sam? Who's Sam?" Eddie asked.

"Sam Zuckert, the promoter who's putting up all the seed money for our band," Brian said. "He's been getting good reports on us, and guess what? He's coming down here to hear us tomorrow night!"

"Oh," Eddie said.

"Well, aren't you excited?" Brian asked.

"Uh, oh yeah." Eddie sounded completely unexcited.

"Oh, don't mind him, I mean, *her*," Frank called from the bathroom. "It always takes a while for good news to sink into that thick skull."

"I see," Brian said. "Well, get some sleep. This could be our big break, but we have to be fantastic tomorrow night."

Brian turned around and left the room. As soon as he was gone, Frank came out of the bathroom.

"You hear that?" Frank asked. "That big hotshot promoter from the city is coming tomorrow night."

"Maybe you guys could do an acoustic set," Eddie said. "You know, a Femme Brigade Unplugged."

"Eddie, you can't quit," Frank said.

Eddie tapped the side of his head with his hand. "Do I hear an echo? Isn't this a conversation we've had, like, two hundred times already?"

"But don't you see?" Frank said. "Now we're on the brink of stardom. This is where you've always wanted to be, dude. You gotta hang in there. You can't let the girls down."

"Give me a break!" Eddie groaned.

"I am totally serious," Frank said.

"That's easy for you to say, Frank," Eddie said. "You don't have some whacko with a knife drooling all over you."

Frank had to think fast. "Okay, okay. You're right. But listen. Give it one more night. Let's show this hotshot promoter what we've got. Once he's gone, you can go too. Because if he likes the band we can always get another drummer. We just can't do it between now and tomorrow night."

Eddie pulled off the blond wig and ran his hand over his smooth head. "Listen, Frank. You and I both know we've been here before. We've had guys from the city come to hear us. Then they go back to the city and we never hear from them again. Just because some guy comes don't mean nothin'. It's a long way between that and some record company gettin' behind a band."

"But it's still a chance," Frank said. "Maybe we had chances before and they didn't come through. But that don't mean the next one won't. You know what'll happen if this one comes through? You get a gig as a drummer."

"A *girl* drummer," Eddie said.

"Hey, I'll let you in on a little secret," Frank said. "If this band gets big, it ain't gonna matter anymore. You can tell everyone you've decided to have a sex change operation. It'll just make more people come to see us."

Eddie pulled off the turtleneck and unhooked his padded bra.

"You know, you kill me, Frank. This don't have anything to do with the band makin' it or not. This is all about Sabrina. Man, who'd ever believe this? That Frank Strone the lady-killer—Use 'em and lose 'em Frank—would be so stuck on some chick that he'd run around pretending to be a girl just to stay near her."

Frank crossed his arms and leveled his gaze at his friend. "I've told you a hundred times, Eddie. This isn't about grabbing some tail. It isn't about a fling. This is like Romeo and Juliet, man. It *transcends* everything that's ever happened before."

Eddie studied him closely. "Do you know what you're talkin' like, man? You're talkin' like this is forever. You're talkin' like"—Eddie had a pained look—"marriage or something."

"Could be, Eddie," Frank said.

"Frank, you're seventeen," Eddie said. "You feelin' okay?"

Frank nodded. "You gotta do what you gotta do. You know what would happen if I let Sabrina slip through my fingers? I'd spend the rest of my life regretting it. I told you, dude, this is a once-in-a-lifetime thing."

"How can you *know* something like that?" Eddie asked.

"Look," Frank said, "remember what you called me before? 'Use 'em and lose 'em' Strone? Well, you're right. I'm seventeen, and I've met a lot of girls, but there's something different about Sabrina. There's something special about her. She's like pure, she's perfect, she's—"

"Okay, okay, I get the picture," Eddie said. "She's the once-in-a-lifetime babe. Just remember, it's gonna be a real short lifetime once Sharkbait Joe figures out what's goin' down."

"I'll take my chances," Frank said. "So how about it, Eddie? Hang in a little longer?"

Eddie sat down on the bed. His shoulders slumped forward and he shook his head. "How'd I ever get myself into this? I gotta dress like a girl all day long. I got Toni who wants to go out drinkin' and fightin' every night. I got some knife-wielding killer in love with me . . . "

Frank sat down next to him on the bed and put his arm around his shoulder. "Just think, someday you'll have great stories to tell your grandkids."

"If I live that long," Eddie muttered.

THE NEXT DAY WAS THE SAME THING as usual. Sleep late, rehearse, and head for the Surfside. Everyone was excited about Sam Zuckert coming.

"This could be it," said Ann, the tall bass player. "This could really be it."

"Everybody calm down," said Brian, who looked like he was the most excited of all. "Now remember, we gotta be super tight tonight. Everyone's just gotta be great."

Sabrina and Frank were sitting together on the couch. Sabrina reached for Frank's hand.

"I'm so nervous, Frankie," she whispered.

"Don't worry, you'll be great," Frank whispered and squeezed her hand.

Sabrina looked down at their hands and frowned. "What happened to your hands?"

Frank didn't follow. "I don't know, what?"

"The nails," Sabrina said.

"Oh . . . " After the night he'd taken the polish

off, Frank had forgotten to paint his nails again. "They, uh, they were really pretty, but I just wasn't comfortable. You know, just a little too flashy for me."

"Oh, Frankie . . . " Sabrina patted his hand. "That's okay. I understand."

The dressing room door opened, and Grungy Arnie came in carrying a wreath of flowers.

"Hey, I'm sorry, no visitors before the show," Brian said.

"I'm just deliverin' some flowers from Joe," Arnie sneered. "For the band."

Since it was a gift for the band, Brian let Arnie in. Arnie set the wreath down. It was a bunch of flowers in the shape of a broken leg.

"Look," Toni said. "There's a card."

She stood up and opened the envelope. "To the best girl band in the world," she read. "Good luck tonight and break a leg."

While the other girls oohed and ahhed over the flowers, Grungy Arnie stepped over to Frank and Eddie.

"I talked to Sal," he said in a low voice. "Turns out he don't know nothin' about two girl musicians from Clotsburg named Frankie and Ellie."

Eddie gave Frank a nervous glance.

"Well," Frank said. "I guess we're just not the memorable types."

"The funny thing is, he does know two guys," Arnie said. "One's a tall guitar player named Frank. The other's a short stocky drummer named Eddie. And you wanna know what's really strange?"

Frank and Eddie nodded slowly.

"Neither of 'em's been around Clotsburg for the last couple of weeks," Arnie said. "Which is about the same amount of time you girls have been here."

"Well, that certainly is a coincidence," Frank said and turned to Eddie. "Wouldn't you say so, Ellie?"

"Oh, yes, Frankie," Eddie nodded and the blond curls of his wig bounced. "That certainly is a coincidence."

Brian came over to Arnie. "Please thank Joe for us and tell him that we love the flowers," he said. "Now I really have to ask you to leave. The girls and I have to get ready."

Arnie nodded and got up, but not before giving Frank and Eddie one last suspicious look. Then he left. Sabrina leaned toward Frank.

"What was *that* all about?" she asked in a low voice.

Frank just shook his head and shrugged. He looked at Eddie. Even under six layers of makeup, his pal looked very pale. Suddenly, Eddie jumped up and ran out the back door. Everyone stared.

"What happened?" Brian asked.

"Must be a case of the nerves," Frank said quickly and raced out the door after him. Outside in the dark, Eddie was running through the parking lot. The curls of his blond wig were flying.

"Oh, Ellie!" Frank yelled in his girl voice and took off after him.

Eddie didn't stop. He took off across the beach. Frank raced after him.

"Ellie!" Frank gasped in the girl voice. "Stop, Ellie!"

Eddie didn't stop, but he did slow down as he struggled through the loose sand.

"Eddie!" Frank yelled again

Eddie still didn't stop.

"Damn it, Eddie!" Frank shouted in his real voice.

"Forget it, Frank!" Eddie gasped as he struggled through the sand.

Frank was catching up to him.

"It's over!" Eddie yelled. "Arnie knows! We're dead men!"

Frank lunged forward.

"*Ooof!*" He tackled Eddie around the ankles and brought him down. They wrestled around in the sand.

"I don't care what you say!" Eddie cried as he struggled. "I don't care what you do! I ain't goin' back!"

Finally, Frank got him in a headlock.

"Ow!" Eddie squirmed around but couldn't get loose. "Ow! You're hurting me!"

"You gonna listen?" Frank asked.

"It don't matter!" Eddie squirmed. "It's over! Ow! Stop it!"

"Not till you agree to listen," Frank said, keeping a tight grip on Eddie's head.

"Okay, okay, just let go!"

Frank let go. He and Eddie sat on the sand, gasping for breath. They both had sand in their clothes. Eddie's wig was all messed up. He yanked it off and inspected it.

"Now look what you did!" he yelled.

"I thought it didn't matter anymore," Frank said.

"It doesn't!" Eddie threw the wig down on the sand and stood up. He started twisting and shaking himself. "Geez, Frank, now I'm all full of sand."

Frank picked up the blond wig and shook it out. "Listen, it's not as bad as you think."

"Are you crazy?" Eddie asked him. "Arnie knows!"

"Arnie doesn't know," Frank corrected him. "He *suspects*. There's a big difference."

"It ain't gonna seem like a big difference after Joe slices us into little pieces and feeds us to the sharks," Eddie said.

"Arnie's not gonna tell Joe anything," Frank said.

Eddie just stared at him. "What're you talking about?"

"Look, we both know Arnie's dumb," Frank said. "But he's not dumb enough to tell Joe that the girl he's crazy about is really a guy."

"Why not?" Eddie asked.

"Because what do you think Joe would do?" Frank asked.

"He'd probably slice up Arnie and feed *him* to the sharks," Eddie said.

"Exactly," said Frank. "So no matter what Arnie thinks, he's not gonna tell Joe a thing. He's just gonna wait till Joe figures it out himself."

"Great," Eddie muttered. "*Then* he'll slice us up."

"No, man, because you'll be gone by then." Frank handed Eddie the wig.

Eddie looked down at the wig and shook his head. "I can't believe I'm doin' this. I really can't." Then he pulled the wig back on.

"Come on," Frank said. "We gotta get back to the club and get all this sand off before the show."

Frank started back up the beach toward the club.

"I've lost my mind," Eddie grumbled as he followed behind. "I've completely lost my mind."

THE BAND REALLY COOKED THAT night and the audience loved it. Chrissy sang her brains out and the rhythm section of Ann on bass and Eddie on drums was like a steam locomotive. If there was any weakness in the group, it was, unfortunately, Sabrina. She just couldn't quite get down as sweaty and funky as Toni could. It seemed to Frank that she had a certain daintiness and feminine reserve which stopped her from really shaking her stuff. And while that might have hurt her as a backup singer, it was a big part of what had attracted him to her in the first place.

The glare of the spotlights made it impossible for the band to see out into the crowd, but Brian sent word back that Sam Zuckert was indeed out there.

When the gig was finally over, the sweat-soaked band was deluged with the loudest applause they'd ever received. Exhausted but giddy, they left the stage and staggered back to the dressing room. Brian was waiting there for them.

"You were great!" he yelled, hugging Chrissy. "Just fabulous!"

He went around the room and congratulated each of them.

"Now listen," he said. "I've got a special surprise. Sam wants to come back and meet you himself. He only does that when he really, really likes a band. Just wait here and I'll be right back."

Brian went out. Almost immediately, the girls started primping, touching up their makeup and brushing out their hair.

"Quick, I need a hair dryer!" Chrissy gasped.

Someone found her one and she started to blow dry her hair. Meanwhile, Frank and Eddie gave each other looks. Neither of them was much into primping.

"So, uh, how do I look, Frankie?" Eddie asked in a low voice.

"You're okay," Frank replied.

The girls were so busy making themselves up that they didn't seem to notice that Frank and Eddie just stood there. Then the door opened and Brian came in with a small man with short brown hair.

"Everyone," Brain said, "I'd like you to meet Sam."

Frank was surprised. He'd expected some heavyset guy with a dark suit and a fat cigar. But Sam Zuckert was wearing a pair of jeans and a plain plaid shirt with the sleeves rolled up to his forearms.

"I'm delighted to meet you," he said, kissing Toni on both cheeks. "I thought you were fantastic."

Sam went around the room, kissing and congratulating each of them. As he got close to Eddie and Frank, Eddie gave his buddy a nervous look. Neither of them really wanted to be kissed by this guy, but there was nothing they could do. Frank shrugged. Sam turned to Eddie and kissed him on the cheek.

"You are one of the most fabulous drummers I've ever seen!" Sam gushed. "Male or female!"

"Uh, gee, thanks." Eddie grinned proudly.

Sam turned to Frank. He had to get up on his tiptoes and Frank had to bend over. He tried not to wince as Sam kissed him on the cheek. "Excellent guitar playing, just superb."

Sabrina would have been next in line to be congratulated, but Sam turned to Brian and wagged a finger at him. The two men huddled in a corner and talked. Each would occasionally glance back at the band. It was pretty obvious to Frank that Sam was talking about them. He just wished he knew what they were saying.

Finally, Sam returned to the whole group.

"Now listen," he said. "I think you're all fabulous, just fabulous. Just keep doing exactly what you're doing, and I know there'll be big things in your future."

The three nuns held hands and grinned. Toni threw her arms around Sabrina and hugged her. Sam checked his watch.

"Okay, guys, I have to split," he said. "I'll be in touch. Keep up the good work."

Sam turned and went out the door. For a second there was silence in the dressing room. As if no one could believe what had just happened.

Frank turned to Eddie. "You gotta admit, we never had *that* happen before," he whispered.

Eddie just nodded. He seemed dumbstruck.

Ann pressed her hands to her cheeks. "Oh, my God!" she screeched. "Did you hear that? He loved us!"

Everyone started screeching and screaming and running around and hugging each other.

"Hey, wait a minute," Toni said. Everyone stopped.

"If he loved us so much, how come he wants us to stay and play this rinky-dink club?" she asked. "How come he doesn't move us to a bigger club?"

"All in good time," Brian said. "But the good news is the manager here at the Surfside loves you so much that he's extended the band's engagement for another week!"

The girls all looked uncertainly at each other. "Well, I guess that's good news," Rachel said.

"Believe me, it is," Brian said.

"Well, what about those other bands?" Chrissy asked.

"They're still in the running," Brian said. "But frankly, I think we've got the best chance."

"Why?" asked Ann.

"You saw Sam tonight," Brian said. "He loved you."

"How do we know he doesn't say that to all his bands?" Toni asked. "To keep them all hanging on?"

"Because I don't think he has to," Brian said. "I think he tells it like it is. But listen, maybe I'm wrong. We'll know in a week."

"Why?" Eddie asked.

"Because we've got one more week here," Brian said. "If Sam likes us as much as he says he does, he'll line up another gig for us. If he doesn't, it's back to Clotsburg. But, hey, I think you're wrong. I really think you're on your way."

The band looked at each other uncertainly.

"Maybe he's right," Chrissy said. "We have to look at this as a good sign. Let's not turn it into a downer."

"Right," said Ann.

The rest of the band members agreed and the celebration began again. But Frank noticed something odd. Sabrina stood off to the side with her arms crossed and a somber look on her face.

He went over to her.

"Why the long face?" he asked in his girl voice.

Sabrina shrugged and didn't say anything.

"Come on, it's me, Frankie," Frank said. "You can tell me."

Sabrina blinked as if she was fighting back tears. Frank really didn't understand what the problem was.

"Hey, what's wrong?"

Sabrina shook her head. "I don't want to spoil a good time," she whispered. Then she went to the back door and went out. Frank followed her outside. Sabrina stopped in the dark parking lot and pressed her hands to her face and started to sob.

"Whoa . . . " Frank put his arm around Sabrina's shoulder to comfort her. He could feel her tremble as she cried. "Hey, hey, now, what's the problem?"

"He . . . he didn't like me," Sabrina sobbed and sniffed.

"Who?"

"That man," Sabrina said with a quavering voice. "Zuckert."

"Are you kidding?" Frank said. "He loved you. He loved all of us."

"No, Fankie." Sabrina shook her head.

"Sabrina . . . " Frank held her close.

"He . . . he didn't like me," Sabrina said with a tremble. "I could tell."

"How?"

"He went to everyone else and kissed them," Sabrina sniffed. "He told them how much he liked their music. But he didn't say anything to me. He ignored me."

"Aw, come on," Frank said. "You saw him look at his watch. He was just in a rush. If he didn't get to you, you shouldn't take that personally."

Sabrina shook her head. "Remember when they went into the corner to talk in private? They were talking about me."

"How do you know?" Frank asked.

"Because Brian kept looking at me with this guilty look on his face," she said.

"You don't know for sure," Frank said.

"Yes I do, Frankie," she insisted.

"I'm telling you you're wrong," Frank said. "You're great. There's nothing about you that he couldn't like. You're sweet and sensitive and nice. I think you're fantastic!"

Sabrina smiled up at him through her tears. "Thanks, Frankie, that's nice to hear. But sweet and sensitive isn't what they want from a backup singer. They want you to be sexy and wild, and that's just not my style."

Sabrina looked away. Frank took her chin in his hand and turned her back toward him.

"Everybody has their own style," he said in his girl voice. "They don't expect you to be just like Toni. You have to be yourself. And really, I think you're fabulous, just being you."

"But I'm not even a very good singer," Sabrina said.

"Hey, you're great, just fine," Frank said.

"Maybe I should just go home," Sabrina said.

"No!" Frank gasped, then caught himself. "Come on, kid, you're part of the band. We all love you. We're all together in this. Nobody wants to see you go."

Sabrina rubbed her eyes and gazed up at him with a searching, innocent expression on her face. "Do you really mean it?"

Frank looked down at her and nodded. She looked so innocent, so vulnerable. He could feel that magnetism welling inside him. Their faces were close, her lips were only inches from his. He wanted to take her in his arms, hold her and kiss her and never let anything bad happen to her. He moved his face a little closer to hers. She was still looking up at him with that open, unguarded look. He felt his lips moving closer to hers. He knew he shouldn't. She thought he was Frankie, the girl. What would she think? But the desire was too strong. He couldn't help himself.

"There you guys are!"

Frank jumped back as Sharkbait Joe came out the door of the dressing room.

"I WONDERED WHAT HAPPENED TO you two." Sharkbait joined them. It was obvious to Frank that either he hadn't noticed how close he and Sabrina were or didn't care because he thought Frank was a girl.

"So what's up?" Sharkbait asked. "What're you doing out here?"

"Frankie and I were just talking," Sabrina said.

"Oh, yeah?" Sharkbait said. "That's good. It's good you got a girlfriend like Frankie you can talk to."

Frank nodded and wondered how Joe would feel if he knew who Frankie really was. He'd probably throw a fit from here to Hoboken and then slice Frank into pieces so small they'd need tweezers to pick up all the parts.

Sharkbait put his arm around Sabrina. "I'm glad you got a good friend, Sabrina, cause I gotta go away for a while."

"Where?" Sabrina asked.

"Up to the city," Sharkbait said. "I got some business to attend to."

"What kind of business is that?" Frank asked innocently.

"The kind of business that's no one else's business," Joe said with a smile. "The trouble is, I don't know how long it's gonna take. Could be a couple of weeks, could be longer."

"Oh, that's really too bad," Frank said in his girl voice. Actually, it was the best news he'd heard in weeks!

"But I don't want you to worry," Joe said to Sabrina. "I know Frankie here will take good care of you. And I told Arnie to hang around too, just to keep an eye on things."

Crap, Frank thought.

"So, uh, I just wanna say good-bye," Joe said.

"You mean, you're leaving right now?" Frank didn't want to sound too excited.

"Yeah, gotta head up there tonight," Joe said.

"Too bad," Frank said.

Joe glanced at Sabrina and then back at Frank. "So listen, Frankie, maybe you could leave us alone for a little while, okay."

"Uh, okay." Frank hated to do it, but he went through the back door and into the dressing room again.

Inside, the girls were still partying. Some fans, mostly girls, had come in. Eddie was talking to two girls Frank had never seen before.

"I think a lot of drummers make that mistake," Eddie was saying in his girl voice. "They just keep adding drums and cymbals instead of working on technique. They've never figured out that it's really the drummer and not the drum set that makes the sound."

The girls nodded. Frank could see they were really impressed.

"You know who Charlie Watts is?" Eddie asked.

The girls shook their heads.

"The drummer for the Rolling Stones," Eddie said. "Probably one of the greatest rock and roll drummers who ever lived. He had great technique, great sound, and he did it all with a snare, a high hat, a bass, one tom tom, a ride and a crash."

"That's all?" Both girls looked surprised. Frank could only assume they were both aspiring drummers.

"Yeah, he didn't need all that other stuff," Eddie said. "Just the basics and he was great."

"How did you get to be so good?" one of the girls asked.

"Practice," Eddie replied. "Practice and a certain amount of innate talent."

Frank rolled his eyes. Eddie was really eating this star stuff up.

"I've always admired your innate talent too, Ellie," Frank said, batting his eyes.

Eddie gave him a sour look.

"I'm sorry," Frank said to Eddie's fans. "You think I could borrow this incredibly talented drummer girl for a second?"

The girls nodded. Frank led Eddie away.

"Hey, what's with you?" Eddie asked.

"Innate talent?" Frank asked, with a smile.

"Hey, I got a right to talk to girls," Eddie said.

"Just don't forget that they think you're a girl too," Frank said. "You go putting the moves on them and they might get the wrong idea."

"I'll try to keep that in mind," Eddie said. "So I saw you follow Sabrina outside before. What's the story?"

Frank told him about Sabrina being upset and thinking she wasn't good enough.

"I hate to tell you this, but she's right," Eddie said. "You're up front playin' guitar so you don't see what I see from the back. She's stiff *and* she doesn't hit her notes. Now you and I know that it's okay to be stiff if you hit your notes. And if you're a real hot fox, it's okay to miss a note here or there. But it ain't good when you're missing on both counts."

Frank nodded. He had a feeling Eddie was right. Then he told him about Joe going away and leaving Arnie around.

"It's 'cause Arnie's suspicious," Eddie said. "He knows something's goin' on even if he can't tell Joe what it is. He knows that if he goes to the city with Joe and you run off with Sabrina and they find out I'm a guy, Joe's gonna have a fit to end all fits. And sooner or later he's gonna blame Arnie for it."

Frank nodded. He knew his friend was right.

The back door opened and Sabrina and Sharkbait Joe came in. Brian came over and told Sabrina he had to talk to her in private. As soon as they were gone, Joe came over to Frank and Eddie.

"So how's my favorite drummer?" he asked.

"Just swell, Joe, how about you?" Eddie replied in his girl voice as he twirled a finger in his blond wig curls.

"Eh, not so good," Joe said. "Frankie tell you I gotta go away?"

"Oh, no!" Eddie pretended to be upset.

"Yeah, I gotta," Joe said. "So listen, I want you to take care of yourself while I'm gone, you hear? I wanna make sure you're still around when I get back."

"Oh, you can count on it," Eddie said and winked his false eyelashes.

"Good, good." Joe gave Eddie an odd look from his head to his toes, then walked away.

As soon as he was gone, Eddie turned to Frank. "What was that look he just gave me?"

"Well, I can't say for sure," Frank said with a grin. "But if I had to guess, I'd say he just undressed you with his eyes."

Eddie pressed his fingers against his temples and shook his head. "I gotta get out of here."

"Hey, you always wanted to get a shot at the big time," Frank reminded him. "It looks like you might get it. You really gonna quit now?"

"The big time ain't gonna do me any good if I'm a corpse, which is what I'm gonna be sooner or later," Eddie said.

"Look, Joe's gonna be gone for a few weeks," Frank said. "On the other hand, we ought to know what's gonna happen with this band by the end of the week. At least hang in until then."

Eddie gazed across the room to where

Grungy Arnie was sitting in a chair with his arms crossed over his big belly. Arnie was watching them with a squint. Eddie looked back at Frank.

"Do me a favor, Frankie, don't use that word, hang," Eddie said. "It reminds me too much of how I'm probably gonna end up."

The door opened and Sabrina came back in, looking somber. Brian followed her, not looked particularly happy himself. When Sabrina saw Frank, she nodded at him knowingly.

"Okay, girls," Brian slapped his hands together. "Let's get out to the van. It's time to head back to the motel."

They went out and climbed into the van. As usual, Frank sat with Sabrina. He leaned over and whispered into her ear. "What'd Brian have to say?"

"He gave me a warning," Sabrina whispered back.

Frank frowned. "What kind of warning?"

"I'll tell you, but you have to promise not to tell anyone," Sabrina said. "Not even Ellie."

"Okay."

Sabrina took a deep breath and let it out slowly. "Brian said either I have to shape up or ship out."

Frank gave Sabrina a surprised look, but Sabrina only nodded back sadly. Her expression said, *I told you.*

IT WAS LATE WHEN THEY GOT BACK to the motel. Frank and Eddie went into their room, but it wasn't long before there was a knock on the door.

"Who is it?" Eddie asked in his girl voice. His blond wig lay on the bed beside him.

"Toni and Sabrina."

Eddie glanced at Frank and whispered, "I can't do this anymore. These late nights going out drinking are killing me."

"You have to," Frank said. "I really have to talk to Sabrina tonight."

"Can't you talk to her tomorrow?"

"When?" Frank asked. Tomorrow they would wake up, have breakfast, and start rehearsing for that night's show.

"Jeez, man, what's so important?" Eddie asked.

"I can't tell you," Frank said. "It's a secret."

"What is this?" Eddie asked. "Now you and her got secrets?"

"Just one," Frank said. "But she made me promise."

Toni tapped on the door again. "Ellie? It's time to go. You comin'?"

Eddie gave Frank a look. Frank gave him an urgent nod.

"Okay," Eddie said in his girl voice. "Just give me a second."

Eddie pulled on his wig and went to the bathroom and touched up his makeup. Then he headed for the door.

"See ya later," he grumbled.

"Hey," Frank said. "Don't do anything I wouldn't do."

"I can't," Eddie replied. "As long as I have to be a girl, I ain't got the equipment."

Eddie opened the door and Sabrina came in while he went out. Toni stuck her head in.

"So what are you two going to do tonight?" she asked Frank and Sabrina.

"Just talk," Sabrina said.

"Ooh-wee, sounds exciting." Toni winked and left.

They left and Sabrina sat down on the corner of Frank's bed. Her shoulders slumped.

Frank had an idea. "Hey, I know what!"

Sabrina looked up. "What?"

"Why don't we practice?" he said, shimmying a little. "Like getting you loose."

But Sabrina shook her head. "I know what I have to do, Frankie. It's just . . . "

"Just what?"

"It's just hard to do it in front of a crowd," Sabrina said. "I don't know how Toni can be so uninhibited."

"I guess that's just the way she is," Frank said.

Sabrina glanced back at the door. "You know, it's a beautiful night out. There's a full moon. Want to go for a walk?"

"Where?" Frank asked.

"Just along the road."

"What about Brian?"

"I think Brian has his milk and cookies and goes beddy-bye every night," Sabrina said with a smile and a wink.

It wasn't long before they were strolling down the road away from the motel. The air was cool and crisp, and the moon was a great big glowing orb in the sky.

"I love going outside on a full moon," Sabrina said.

"They used to make people wear hats," Frank said.

"Huh?" Sabrina gave him a puzzled look.

"They used to believe that if you went outside on a full moon with a bare head you'd get crazy," Frank said. "You know the word lunacy?"

"Yes."

"Well, luna is the latin word for the moon," Frank said. "Lunacy comes from the belief that going outside under a full moon made people crazy."

Sabrina gave him a look. "You took Latin?"

"Naw," Frank grinned. "It was just one of

those weird things that's always stuck in my head, you know?"

Sabrina nodded. "Yeah. It's like the life cycle of the cicada."

"The what?" Frank frowned.

"Those big bugs that fly around and make that loud whiny noise in the summer," Sabrina said. "Some of them live underground for as long as fifteen years. Then they finally get to come out into the sun and mate. But after that they only live for a couple of days. I always thought that was so sad."

"Like spending all that time in the dark and dirt?" Frank guessed. "And then when you're finally free you have to die?"

Sabrina nodded.

"Yeah," Frank said. "That is pretty sad."

"Sometimes I feel that way," Sabrina said, looking down at the cans and dirt along the side of the road.

"Like you're gonna die?" Frank asked.

"No, Frankie." She flashed a smile at him. "Like I'm kind of stuck in the dark, yearning to break free."

"But you are free," Frank said.

Sabrina shook her head. "I feel trapped. I'm trapped in this thing with Joe. Sometimes I feel trapped in this band."

"I thought you loved it," Frank said.

"Yes and no. I mean, it's the same thing night after night. I can see how it gets old after a while."

"Not to me," Frank said. "Every night it's a little different. You can play a riff a little different, do a song a little different."

"That proves my point," Sabrina said. "You see, you're a real musician, Frankie, so that's fun for you. For me every night's like homework. It's like trying to remember what to do when and praying I get it right. To be honest, it's really not as much fun as I thought it would be."

"You sure you're not just saying that as a defense?" Frank asked. "Because you're afraid you're gonna get canned and you're coming up with an excuse already?"

"Maybe there's a little of that," Sabrina said. "But it almost doesn't matter, you know. If it's meant to be, then it'll be."

"So you really believe in fate, huh?" Frank asked.

"Sort of," Sabrina said. "I don't believe that things are planned out in advance for us. But I do believe that certain things happen because the pieces fit, and certain things don't happen because the pieces don't fit."

"So what about you and Joe?" Frank asked.

Sabrina stopped. She crossed her arms in front of her and looked up at the moon.

"I think it's just a step on a ladder," she said. "It's not the goal. He sort of helped me get going, and for that I owe him my thanks."

Frank stopped near her. "What's the goal?" he asked.

Sabrina sighed. "I'd like to fall in love. I know that sounds hokey, but it's true. Have you ever been in love, Frankie?"

Frank nodded. "Yeah."

"What was he like?"

"It's hard to explain," Frank said. "It was this person and the second I saw her I just knew that she was the—"

Suddenly he noticed that Sabrina had turned and was staring at him in the dark.

"Her?" she said.

"Uh . . . is that what I said?" Frank asked.

Sabrina nodded.

"Well, er, I really meant—"

Sabrina smiled. "No you didn't, Frankie. You really meant her. It's okay. I had a feeling."

Frank's eyes widened. "You did?"

Sabrina nodded. She reached toward him and put her hand on his shoulder. "I mean, look at you. You're built like a guy, you move like a guy. I don't mind. I just feel a little sad for you."

"Why?" Frank asked, completely bewildered.

"Well, it must be hard," Sabrina said. "I mean, sometimes I look at you, and it's like I see this guy in a girl's body just yearning to break out. And no matter what anyone says, society doesn't really accept you, does it?"

"Well, uh . . . " Frank still didn't know what to say.

"Ellie's one too, isn't she?" Sabrina asked.

"Uh, Ellie?"

Sabrina smiled. "It's okay. I won't tell anyone if you don't want me to. You kept my secret and I'll keep yours."

"Oh, yeah, thanks." Frank wasn't certain what all this meant.

"So you saw her and you knew right away," Sabrina said. "What was she like?"

"It's . . . it's hard to explain," Frank said. "I just saw her and knew. She was so pretty and delicate and . . . sweet and nice. And you could just tell right away that she was the one."

"Did you talk to her?"

"Yeah," Frank said. "I talked to her a lot."

"And?"

Frank just shrugged. "She doesn't really know how I feel."

"You mean, she not . . . like you?" Sabrina guessed.

Frank shook his head slowly.

"Oh, Frankie, that's so sad," Sabrina said, stroking his head. "I mean, isn't there a chance she's, uh, you know?"

"I really doubt it," Frank said. "But that's okay."

"No, it's not!" Sabrina gasped. "How can you say that? It's incredibly sad."

"Well, I accept that that's the way it is," Frank said. "At least for now."

Sabrina frowned. "You mean, you think maybe she'll change?"

"I don't know what will happen," Frank said. "I just have hope. It's what gets me through every day."

Sabrina just gazed sadly at him.

"Hey, don't feel sorry for me," Frank said. "I've learned to live with it. It's okay. But let's talk about you. What do you imagine your ideal guy will be like?"

Sabrina grinned. "Well, he'll be a musician. Probably a guitar player."

Frank was shocked. "Why?"

"Well, I guess because I really admire people who are good at music," Sabrina said. "And he'll be sensitive and funny and a good listener. And he'll be understanding, and he won't be demanding, and he'll just be really easy and comfortable to be with."

Frank stared down at the ground and nodded. When he looked back up, Sabrina was staring at him.

"What?" he asked.

"You know what I just realized?" Sabrina asked.

Frank shook his head.

"He'll be just like you, Frankie." Sabrina reached out and took his hand. "Isn't this sad? We'd be perfect for each other . . . if only you were a guy."

Frank felt his eyes lock into hers. *If he were a guy . . .* Oh, man, it would be so easy. He could do it right then and there. But he couldn't do it to the band. And he couldn't do it while Grungy Arnie was still hanging around . . . Somehow he had to force himself to wait.

"I think we better go back," he said.

Sabrina nodded. "Okay."

They started back down the road. Frank couldn't believe how close he was, yet how far he had to go.

THE BAND PLAYED HARD AND WELL all week. Frank stayed close to Sabrina, but Grungy Arnie was always hanging around. Sabrina did her best to get down and dirty during the shows, but Frank could tell that Brian still wasn't happy. Meanwhile they waited for a word about the future.

Finally the word came. It was the afternoon before their final gig at the Surfside Club. Brian called everyone into his motel room.

Frank, Eddie, Toni, and Sabrina got there first.

"So what's the story, Brian?" Toni asked.

"I want to wait until everyone's here before I tell," Brian said.

"Is it good news or bad?" Eddie asked.

"It's, uh, great news," Brian said. Then he glanced out of the corner of his eye at Sabrina and added, "Mostly."

The three nuns came into the room, looking

both apprehensive and excited. Brian closed the door behind them.

"Okay, girls," he said, "Sam just called."

"And?" Chrissy asked eagerly.

"He . . . " Brian gave it a dramatic pause, then grinned. "He's booked us to play a week at Trax, started the night after next."

"Trax in the city!?" Chrissy squealed.

Brian nodded. "You're on your way, girls."

Everyone went crazy, screaming and yelling and hugging each other. They started jumping on the beds and throwing pillows. It degenerated into a pillow fight and lasted until one of the pillows broke and showered them all with a fine snow of down. Then everyone slumped down in chairs and on the floor, exhausted.

"There you go," Brian groaned. "You get your first big break and you start acting like a famous rock band, trashing motel rooms."

Ann held up one of the feathers. "How come none of us have down pillows in our rooms?"

"I brought that from home," Brian said. "It was my favorite pillow."

"Aw, we didn't know," said Toni, giving him a hug.

"Yeah, we never would have destroyed it if we knew it was your favorite pillow," said Eddie in his girl voice.

"Hey, it's okay," said Brian. "I can always get another one."

After that, the celebration broke up and everyone went back to their rooms to start preparing for the last show at the Surfside that night. But as Sabrina left the room, Brian asked her to stay behind.

Sabrina gave Frank a sad look as if to say, *This is it.*

Frank went out and closed the door behind him. But then he stood outside Brian's room.

"What're you waiting for?" Eddie asked.

"Brian's talking to Sabrina."

"You want me to wait with you?" Eddie asked.

"No, you go ahead," Frank said.

He didn't have to wait very long. Soon the door opened and Sabrina came out looking crushed. Frank glanced into the room and saw Brian sitting on his bed with his hands clasped in front of him and his lips pursed. He looked up and his eyes met Frank's. Brian shook his head slowly.

Frank pulled the door closed and started to walk with Sabrina.

"Well, have a good time in the city," she said with a sniff.

"What'd he say?" Frank asked.

"They're replacing me," Sabrina said. "Tonight's my last show."

"That twerp." Frank glared back at Brian's room and clenched his fist. "Want me to talk to him?"

Sabrina slid her hand through his arm. "No. Thanks, Frankie, but it's okay."

"Okay?" Frank said. "How can you say that? Being a singer is all you ever wanted to be."

"That's what I thought," Sabrina said. "But after these past few weeks, maybe I've realized that maybe I was wrong. I mean, maybe it was just a dream, but the truth is that I'm not very good. I can't hit the notes and I can't get down and dirty, so maybe it's just not right for me."

"But what'll you do?" Frank asked.

"Oh, I don't know." Sabrina shrugged. "It's beautiful over at the beach. Maybe I'll stay around and get a waitressing job."

"What about Joe?" Frank asked.

"I'll deal with him," Sabrina said. "It won't be the first time I broke up with someone."

They stopped outside Sabrina's room. Sabrina turned to Frank with a crooked smile on her face. "I have to tell Toni," she said. "Listen, Frankie, you've been a really great friend. More than anyone in this band, I'll miss you."

Sabrina stood up on her tiptoes and kissed him on the cheek. Then she went into her room and closed the door.

Frank just stood there and stared at the door for a while. Then he wandered down to his room and went in. He felt like he was in a daze, uncertain what to do. The room was empty.

"Eddie?" Frank said, looking around.

"In here." Eddie came out of the bathroom, fixing his wig. "Can you believe it, dude? Trax! You know what that means?"

Still in a daze, Frank shook his head.

"The big time, dude," Eddie said. "Everyone knows Trax is the launching pad. It's where all the big producers bring their new acts when they're ready to sign with a major label. All the top record guys hang out there. We've made it, Frank! You understand? We've made it!"

Frank just slumped down on the bed. He had to think.

"Hey, what's with you?" Eddie sat down on the bed across from him.

"Sabrina just got canned," Frank said. "Tonight's her last show."

"Hey, that's too bad," Eddie said. "But you can't say it's a shock. We knew it might be coming."

"Yeah." Frank nodded.

"Just think, dude," Eddie said. "Two nights from tonight we'll be playing in the city! The big time! This is a dream come true!"

"Yeah."

Eddie reached over and grabbed Frank by the shoulders. "Hey, Frank, buddy, you gotta snap out of it!"

Frank just stared at his friend. "Suppose I get into my clothes. Suppose I go over to her room right now and show her I'm a guy."

Eddie sat back and looked stunned. "Oh, great. That's just what we need. Two days before we hit the big time, our lead guitarist reveals that he's actually a guy."

"There are a lot of guitar players, Eddie," Frank said. "They'll find someone to take my place."

"Not a lot of good guitarists," Eddie said. "This ain't like replacing a backup singer, dude. Ain't nobody around, male or female, who can step into your shoes and learn all your chops in just two days. You tell everyone you're a guy now and you can kiss this band good-bye. You can kiss Trax good-bye. You're gonna burst the bubble for everyone."

"Gee, thanks, Eddie," Frank said.

"Hey, I'm just telling it like it is, dude," Eddie said. "Just the way you've been telling me for the past month. And even if they could find someone to replace you, where would that leave me? I'd be the only guy in an all-girl band. They'd figure out I was a guy in no time. This is a once-in-a-lifetime opportunity, dude. You quit now and you screw it up for everybody."

He was right. Frank knew it. "But what about Sabrina?"

"She ain't goin' far," Eddie said. "You'll be able to find her."

"But you don't understand," Frank said. "She's gonna break up with Joe. A girl like that won't stay available for long."

Eddie stared at him and shook his head. "I can't believe this is Frank Strone I hear talking. Frank the lady-killer."

"I can't lose this girl," Frank said.

"Nobody said you would," Eddie said. "I mean, you really think she'll run off with the first guy who comes along? What kind of girl do you think she is?"

Frank didn't know if Eddie was right or not. It was a hard situation to call. When it came to things that were truly precious, no one wanted to take any risks.

"And let me tell you something else," Eddie went on. "Maybe she likes you as Frankie, but what makes you so sure she's gonna like you as Frank? I know you think she's the most fabulous girl who ever walked the face of the earth, but maybe she's got a thing for scrawny tattooed guys who carry knives."

"You forget I've already met her as Frank," Frank said. "That night on the beach. I'm pretty sure she liked me."

"Well, you never know," Eddie said.

In a way, Frank knew Eddie was right. You never knew. But he would have to find out . . . soon.

22

THE BAND WAS IN A SOMBER MOOD that night. Maybe it was because they were preoccupied with thinking about what was to come. Or maybe they felt bad for Sabrina. They put on a good show, but not a great one.

Frank thought Sabrina was very brave. She went out of her way to make sure no one felt sorry for her. Frank was proud of her. As soon as the show ended she started to leave the club. Frank caught up to her.

"Where're you going?" he asked in his girl voice.

"I don't want to hang around in the dressing room," she said. "It'll just bring everyone down."

"So what are you gonna do?" Frank asked.

"I thought I'd ask Arnie to take me back to the motel," Sabrina said. "I'll pack up my stuff, and tomorrow morning I'll start looking for a job and a new place to live."

Frank had to think fast. "Just give me a second. I'll come with you."

"That's sweet, Frankie," Sabrina said. "But you don't have to. I'll be okay."

"But I want to come," Frank said. He pretended to yawn. "I'm tired. I really need to get some sleep."

"Well, okay, I'll wait for you outside," Sabrina said.

Frank hurried into the dressing room to get his guitar. When he got there, Eddie sidled up to him.

"What are you up to?" he whispered.

"I'm goin' back to the motel with Sabrina," Frank said. "Do me a favor, okay? Try to get the band to hang around here for a while. Try to keep 'em from going back to the motel as long as possible."

"Why?" Eddie asked.

"Just do it." Frank reached into his pocket and pulled out some money. "Take this and buy everyone a drink at the bar."

Eddie took the money and shoved it into his pocket. "What're you going to do, Frank?"

"I'm not sure yet," Frank said. "That's why I need time."

He picked up his guitar case and went out into the club. Sabrina was waiting there with Grungy Arnie, who gave Frank a withering look.

"Arnie said he'll give us a ride to the motel," Sabrina said.

"That's nice." Frank reached forward and took Arnie's fat cheek between his thumb and forefinger and squeezed. "You're so sweet."

"Lay off," Arnie grumbled.

No one said a word in the car back to the motel. Now Frank knew what he had to do. When they got there, he got out of the car, said good-bye to Sabrina, and went into his room. Inside he quickly changed into his real clothes. Then he went to the door and opened it a hair to peek out.

Darn it! Grungy Arnie was sitting in his car, parked right outside Sabrina's room. Frank closed the door and looked around. He had to find another way to get out. He remembered the window in the bathroom that looked out behind the motel. He went into the bathroom and studied the window. It looked like a tight squeeze, but he had no choice.

Frank quickly took off the screen, then he climbed up on the toilet and got one leg out the window. He managed to get the other leg out and then started to inch his way backward and outside. A few moments later he hit the ground and dusted off his hands. The moon was out, and even though it was only half-full there was enough light for him to see. He went along the back wall of the motel, down two windows and came to the one that should have been Sabrina's bathroom.

Her window was open and covered by the screen. Frank could hear music coming from a radio inside. He stretched up and peeked in. The bathroom door was open and he could see into the bedroom. Lying on the bed was an open suitcase with clothes in it. Then Sabrina came into view as she put a pair of jeans in the suitcase.

"Sabrina!" Frank hissed.

She didn't hear him. The music must've drowned out his voice. Frank waited until she came into view again.

"*Sabrina!*" he gasped.

Sabrina looked up and scowled as if she'd heard something but couldn't tell from where.

"*The bathroom,*" Frank hissed.

Somewhat warily, Sabrina approached the bathroom and looked around.

"*Outside the window,*" Frank whispered.

Sabrina came to the window and peered out. Her jaw dropped when she saw him out there in the dark. "What are you doing here?"

"It's a long story," Frank said. "Listen, can you come out? I have to talk to you."

"How did you find me?" Sabrina hesitated.

"That's part of the long story," Frank said.

"Why can't you come around to the front?" Sabrina asked.

"I can't let Arnie see me," Frank said.

"You know him?"

"Sure. Remember back in Clotsburg?"

"Oh, right," Sabrina said. "Of course."

"So listen, I really need to talk to you," Frank said. "Just take off the screen and climb out."

"Well, I don't know," Sabrina said cautiously. "This is kind of weird. Maybe we should just talk like this."

Frank didn't like that. What he had to say was too important. "Normally, I'd say sure, but I have something real important I gotta say."

"Well, I'm sorry, but I really don't want to climb out the bathroom window," Sabrina said. "I think you should just tell me."

"Sabrina, believe me, this isn't the right way to do it," Frank said.

"Do what?" Sabrina asked.

"Tell you what I gotta tell you."

"I don't understand how it can be that important," Sabrina said. "I mean, I hardly know you."

"That's what you think," Frank said.

"What do you mean?" Sabrina asked.

Frank took a deep breath and then spoke in his girl voice. "Remember that night on the beach? Remember we talked about those two people on that other planet?"

Sabrina's eyes widened as she stared through the screen at him. "I . . . I don't understand."

"There's never been a Frankie," Frank said in his girl voice. Then he switched to his boy voice. "Just Frank."

"*Ahhhh!*" Sabrina screamed.

23

"***SHHHHHH!*** **SABRINA! ARNIE'LL HEAR** you," Frank hissed.

"You're Frankie?" Sabrina gasped.

"Yeah, like I said, it's a long story," Frank said. "I—"

Bang! Bang! He was interrupted by the sound of someone banging on the door to Sabrina's room. "Sabrina? You okay? What's goin' on in there?" It was Arnie.

Sabrina, wide-eyed, looked back at the door and then at Frank.

"Whatever you do," Frank said in a calm voice, "don't tell him about me."

Sabrina looked uncertain. Then she nodded. "Wait here."

She left the bathroom and went to the door. Frank listened as she explained to Arnie that she thought she'd seen a mouse. A moment later she closed the door and came back to the bathroom and looked through the screen at him.

"You were pretending to be Frankie all this time?" She'd obviously calmed down. Unfortunately, she sounded angry. "You tricked me!"

"I didn't have any choice," Frank said. "I wanted to see you, but Joe wanted to kill me and Brian wanted an all-girl band."

"I can't believe this." Sabrina shook her head in amazement.

"I know it must be a real shock," Frank said.

"I told you things—"

"Not really, Sabrina," Frank said. "Nothing more than what I told you."

"You should've told me," she said.

"I couldn't tell you," Frank said.

"And what about that girl Frankie was crazy about?" Sabrina asked. "You made all that up."

"No." Frank shook his head. "Every word of that was true."

"But that was Frankie."

"No, that was Frank," he said. "I was talking about you."

Sabrina was quiet. Then she said, "I'm sorry, Frank. I have to think about this."

"Okay, but just one thing." Frank pressed his hand against the screen. Sabrina didn't move.

"Hey, come on," Frank said with a smile.

Inside the bathroom, Sabrina slowly lifted her hand and pressed it against his.

"Listen," Frank said, "whatever I did, I did it for you. Okay? And everything I ever said to you about how I felt, whether it came from Frank or Frankie . . . I meant every word."

Sabrina nodded. Then she withdrew her hand from the screen.

"Sabrina?" Frank said.

She stepped back from the window. "I'll talk to you, Frank. Tomorrow. Maybe."

"Don't be like this," Frank said.

"I'm sorry, Frankie, I mean, Frank. But this is a big shock for me."

Frank could feel his insides twisting around. This wasn't working out at all. "Wait, Sabrina . . . "

But she walked out of the bathroom and closed the door behind her.

Frank turned away and trudged along behind the motel back to his room. He didn't know how it had happened, but he had the feeling he'd blown it. Maybe Eddie was right after all. Maybe she just had a thing for scruffy guys with tatoos and knives.

He grabbed the window ledge and started to pull himself back into the bathroom. It wasn't easy. He'd just about gotten halfway through the window when he heard the door to the room open.

"Who cares what Brian says." It was Toni and she was coming into the room! "We don't have a gig tomorrow night. If I want to stay up and have a few beers, that's my God-given right."

"Yeah, but—" Frank heard Eddie say in his girl voice as he followed her in.

"No buts, honey," Toni said. "I'm just gonna use the john and then—"

The door to the bathroom swung open. Frank

froze halfway through the window, then instantly started to inch his way back out. Toni reached for the light switch and flicked it on.

"*Ahhhh!*" For the second time that night, a woman screamed in a bathroom.

Frank quickly turned his face away, hoping she wouldn't recognize him. Toni backed out and slammed the door closed.

"There's someone in there!" Frank heard her shout.

Thunk! Frank slid back out of the bathroom window and hit the ground. He pressed himself against the back wall of the motel and stayed there, crouching down.

"In the bathroom?" he heard Eddie's girl voice.

"I swear," Toni gasped. "I saw it."

"It? Was it a guy or a girl?"

"I couldn't tell," Toni gasped. "It had long hair. I didn't get a good look. Go in and see for yourself."

Outside, Frank heard the bathroom door creak open. He heard Eddie say, "There's no one in there."

"It was halfway out the window," Toni gasped behind him. "Look outside."

A head full of blond curls poked out of the window.

"Down here," Frank whispered.

Eddie looked down and pushed the blond curls out of his eyes. "What're you doing?" he whispered.

"I gotta get back into the room," Frank whispered.

"You can't," Eddie whispered. "Toni's here."

"*I know that!*" Frank hissed. "Get rid of her."

"See anything?" Toni asked behind Eddie.

"Naw, there's nothin'," Eddie replied, ducking back in. "Listen, Toni, I'm really not feeling well. I think it must be my time of the month."

Frank waited outside while Eddie got rid of Toni. A few moments later, Eddie stuck his blond curls out again. "Okay, coast's clear."

"Give me a hand," Frank said, reaching up and starting to pull himself through the window again.

Eddie helped him through. Soon Frank was back in the bathroom, dusting himself off.

"So, what happened?" Eddie asked.

Frank shrugged and went into the bedroom. He sat down on a corner of the bed and felt his shoulders sag. "I don't know. It didn't work the way I planned. Instead of being happy, Sabrina was kind of pissed."

"That's it?" Eddie asked.

"She said she needed time to think," Frank said. "She said we'd talk tomorrow . . . maybe."

"Geez." Eddie sat down on the bed next to him. "That's not so good."

"Tell me about it."

"So what are you gonna do?" Eddie asked.

Frank lifted his head. "About what?"

"About the band."

"Geez, Eddie, I don't know."

"Just remember what I said before," Eddie said. "Everyone's depending on you, dude. This is a once-in-a-lifetime thing. You can't let us down."

"Yeah, Eddie, I know." Frank flopped back on the bed and felt his head sink into the pillow. He felt really tired, but somehow he doubted he'd get much sleep that night.

24

THE SKY WAS STARTING TO TURN light and dawn was approaching when Frank finally fell asleep. Later, he woke to find someone shaking his shoulder.

"Hey, Frank, gotta get up."

Frank opened his eyes and looked up into Eddie's madeup face and the curly blond wig.

"Wha . . . ?"

"Sabrina's outside," Eddie said. "She wants to talk to you."

"Oh." Still half asleep, Frank pulled back the covers and pulled on his jeans and a shirt. He went into the bathroom and splashed some water on his face, and then sort of stumbled toward the door.

"Uh, Frank?" Eddie said.

"Yeah?" Frank stopped.

"Where do you think you're going?"

"To talk to Sabrina."

"Dressed like that? Aren't you forgetting something."

Frank looked down at himself and frowned. "My shoes?"

Eddie shook his head. "Except for Sabrina, everyone still thinks you're a girl."

Frank winced. "I can't dress up like a girl for her, man. Not after all this."

"Why doesn't she come in?" Eddie said. "I'll go out."

"Okay."

Eddie went to the door and opened it. He said something to Sabrina and she came in. She always looked great, but that morning she looked more beautiful than ever.

"See you later," Eddie said, and left, pulling the door closed behind him.

Sabrina stopped and stood in the middle of the room a few feet from Frank. Their eyes met. Frank felt a shiver run through him. Was she gonna tell him this was it? That she never wanted to see him again?

Sabrina's eyes began to glisten with tears. Suddenly she lunged toward him, threw her arms around his neck, and pressed her lips against his.

Frank put his hands on her waist and held her tight. It was amazing, unbelievable, but somehow they'd finally cut through all the garbage. Together at last.

But then Sabrina began to push away from him.

"What?" Frank asked, surprised.

"We can't," Sabrina said.

"What do you mean, we can't?" Frank asked. "We just did."

"You don't understand," Sabrina said.

"What?" Frank asked. "That I'm crazy about you? That you're crazy about me?"

"It's Joe," Sabrina said.

"I can deal with him," Frank said.,

"You can't," Sabrina said. "He'll kill you. Don't you remember the first time we met? He wanted to cut you up for just talking to me. He's insanely jealous."

"Listen, Sabrina," Frank said. "It's a big country. We can go anywhere we like. He won't find us."

"He will," Sabrina said. "I know him. He'll track us down to the ends of the earth. Besides, I won't let you leave the band for me."

"Why not?" Frank asked.

"Because I want you to make it," Sabrina said. "I want the band to make it. I couldn't stand it if I knew it failed because of me."

"It won't fail," Frank said.

"It will if you don't stay and play with them," Sabrina said.

Frank stepped back and stared at her. He couldn't believe it. They'd finally found each other. They were finally together! And she was saying it wouldn't work?

Sabrina came close and slid her arms around his waist and kissed him again. "We have to be patient," she said softly. "We have to wait."

"For what?"

"Until the time is right."

"And what do you and I do until then?" Frank asked.

"We don't have to do anything," Sabrina said. "What we have is real, Frank. It'll still be there when the time is right."

Rap! Rap! Someone knocked on the motel room door.

"Who is it?" Frank asked in his girl voice.

"Hey, Frankie, it's Brian. It's almost checkout time. Get your stuff together and let's go. It's time to head over to the club and pack up the equipment. Then we have to head for the city."

"Okay, just a minute," Frank called in his girl voice. Then he looked back at Sabrina. "I can't believe I have to let you go."

Sabrina pressed her head against his shoulder. "I'm not worried, Frank. I know what I feel for you, and I can feel what you feel for me. I can wait as long as it takes."

She squeezed him hard. Frank took her chin in his hand and tilted her face up toward his. He pressed his lips against hers and they kissed. This was the only thing that mattered. Having her, holding her.

They stayed that way for a long time.

Rap! Rap! "Hey, you guys?" Now it was Eddie outside the door.

Frank looked up. "Yeah?"

"Time to go," Eddie said.

"You better get dressed," Sabrina said. "Want me to help you with your makeup?"

"No, never," Frank replied with a smile. "So what'll you do?"

"I saw some signs in town for girls looking for roommates," she said. "I'll find a place to stay."

"How will I find you?"

"I'll be working at the Clam Shanty," Sabrina said. "I got up early this morning and went looking for a waitressing job."

"The Clam Shanty," Frank repeated.

Rap! Rap! "Hey, Frankie, come on!" It was Eddie.

"Just a second, Ellie," Frank called back. Then he turned to Sabrina again. "I can't believe I have to let you go."

"I know." Sabrina nodded. "I can't believe it either. It just feels so right to be in your arms. Letting go feels so wrong."

"You're sure we can't just run?" Frank asked.

Sabrina nodded. Then she stretched up and kissed him on the lips. "I'll wait for you," she whispered. "I don't care how long it takes."

25

BRIAN DROVE THEM UP TO THE CITY. The seat next to Frank was empty. As they rolled along the highway, he felt someone tap him on the shoulder and turned around in his seat. It was Toni.

"Hey, Frankie, you really miss her, huh?" she said.

Frank shrugged.

"She's a sweet kid," Toni said.

Frank nodded.

"But you know she wasn't really cut out to be a singer," Toni said.

"I guess," replied Frank.

"I hear they already got a new girl waiting for us in the city," Toni said. "She's gonna be onstage with us tomorrow night at Trax."

"Hmmm." If only there was a guitarist waiting for them too, to take his place, Frank thought. It was hard for him to believe that he was still in this band, still dressing up like a girl. How long would this last? When would he finally be able to get out of these clothes and wash the make up off for good?

They spent the night in a cheap hotel and rested up for the big show. The next afternoon they packed their equipment into the van and drove to Trax. They parked outside the stage door and started to unload their equipment.

"Hey, what are you girls doing?" A big guy with a beard came out of the stage door.

Brian turned to him. "We're unloading."

"You're the Femme Brigade, right?" said the bearded guy.

"That's right," Brian said.

"Well, you girls don't have to touch anything," the bearded guy said. "We do all that."

Everyone gave each other amazed looks.

"Finally!" Eddie whispered. "We've got roadies!"

"You girls go inside and get ready for the show," the bearded guy said. "The dressing room's right behind the stage."

Brian led them inside. The band stepped into the dressing room and looked around in wonder. In the center of the room was a large table covered with sandwiches, fresh fruit, and a whole fresh roasted turkey ready to be sliced up. There was a big plastic cooler filled with soda, beer, and bottled water. Several comfortable-looking couches stood here and there, and along the walls were makeup tables with brightly lit mirrors.

"Whoa," Toni cried. "This really *is* the big time!"

The girls walked around, looking at everything in awe. But Frank slumped into a couch, totally unexcited. Eddie slid down next to him.

"Look," he whispered. "I know this ain't where you want to be right now. But it's where you are. For the sake of the rest of us, try to get it together okay?"

Frank nodded. "I'll try, Eddie," he whispered back. "Believe me, I'll try."

By the time the band went on that night, Frank had gotten excited. Writers from *Rolling Stone*, *Interview*, and *Details* had come into the dressing room to talk to the band, and a number of record industry people had come in as well. The question was no longer whether they'd get a record contract or not. Now it was a question of how big the contract would be.

Finally, it was time for the band to go onstage. For a moment they were awestruck by the size of the club. It was probably six times larger than the Surfside, and the crowd was huge. But then they started to play, and it was just like old times. The band cooked and the crowd loved them.

The first set ended and the band returned to the dressing room to relax and cool down before the second show began. Frank stepped into the dressing room and was startled to find it filled with people—friends of the band members, the press, record people.

Frank grabbed a bottle of beer out of the cooler and then noticed a small commotion at the entrance to the dressing room. Sharkbait Joe was standing there with a couple of goons Frank had never seen before.

"I'm telling you, I'm a friend of the band," Joe was saying to a guy from the club who wouldn't let him in the room. "Ask Brian, their manager."

The guy turned to Brian. Behind the guy's back, Joe made a fist that Brian could see.

"You want these guys in?" the Trax guy asked.

Brian swallowed and nodded. Joe and his goons grinned and joined the crowd.

Toni stepped behind Frank and whispered, "What's he doing here?"

The answer was obvious. Sharkbait Joe made a beeline for Eddie. Frank watched as Joe gave Eddie a big hug and led him over to a couch. Eddie gave Frank an apprehensive look as they sat down and Joe started to talk. He kept putting his hand on Eddie's shoulder and whispered stuff in Eddie's ear. It was obvious to Frank what was going on. He could feel himself starting to get angry.

Then Joe put his hand on Eddie's thigh . . .

Slap! Eddie smacked Joe on the face!

"I told you I'm not *that* kind of girl!" Eddie huffed.

The room around them went silent. Everyone was staring at them. Eddie's jaw dropped as he realized what he'd done. He'd hit Sharkbait Joe! Joe looked shocked. A couple of his goons started toward Eddie. It probably didn't matter that they thought he was a girl. *No one* was allowed to hit Joe. Frank slid his hand over the neck of the beer bottle. If there was going to be a fight, he'd use it to bash one of Joe's goons on the head.

The goons got closer. Suddenly the door swung open and Grungy Arnie ran in, breathing hard.

"Boss!" he gasped.

"Not now!" Joe barked.

The goons were almost on top of Eddie. Frank knew this was going to be bad. He and Eddie would be lucky to get out of there alive.

"Hold it!" Joe held up his hand to stop his goons. He looked really pissed. "I'll take care of this."

Joe started to turn back to Eddie, who was biting his red lips nervously.

"She's just a girl," Toni reminded him.

"Yeah," said Joe.

Then . . . he smiled.

"But what a girl," he said with a sigh, giving Eddie a dreamy look.

Frank didn't get it.

"You're right," Joe said to Eddie. "I shouldn't have done that. Not to a nice girl like you."

Everyone looked at each other in stunned silence.

But it pissed Frank off. If Eddie was a nice girl, what did that make Sabrina? Frank marched over to Joe and glowered at him.

"So this is what you do when Sabrina's not around, huh?" he said angrily.

Joe looked up at Frank and frowned. "Get lost."

But Frank had no intention of getting lost. "It just kills me that you'd do that to a girl like her," he said.

"I said, get lost," he growled between clenched teeth.

But Frank was too angry to listen. "Did anyone ever tell you that you were a real dirtbag?"

Frank felt someone nudge him in the side. It was Toni.

"What happened to your voice?" she asked.

"Uh, Frankie, remember who you are," Eddie said nervously in his girl voice.

Frank realized he'd been talking in his guy voice! He spun around and saw the shock of realization in Grungy Arnie's eyes.

Meanwhile, Joe stood up and puffed out his chest. "You know who I am?"

"Yeah, you're a punk with a knife who thinks he's a big shot," Frank said, in his Frankie voice.

Sharkbait Joe's eyes widened and he reached into his vest. Frank pulled his fist back and . . .

"*Stop!*" Eddie jumped between them.

Slap! He slapped Joe on the face again. "I'm ashamed of you! What kind of person are you, fighting with women?"

Joe's jaw dropped. Meanwhile, Eddie spun around and faced Frank.

"And *you*, Frankie!" Eddie said in his girl voice. "Who do you think you are, interfering like that? This is *none* of your business!"

"But Sabrina . . . " Frank stammered.

Eddie turned to Joe and stared at him. "Well?"

Joe nodded sheepishly. "You're right."

"Who's right?" Eddie frowned.

"Her." Joe pointed at Frank.

"I am?" Frank was completely puzzled.

"I gotta tell Sabrina the truth," Joe said. "She's a really nice girl, but"—he turned to Eddie—"she don't hold a candle to you."

"But boss," Arnie gasped.

Everyone turned and looked at him.

"She . . . " Arnie pointed a shaking finger at Eddie. "She's a guy!"

JOE TURNED AND STARED WITH astonishment at Eddie.

Frank sighed wearily and shook his head. *This* was it. Now they were really dead.

Joe walked slowly toward Arnie. The room was so quiet you could hear a guitar pick drop.

"What'd you say?" Joe asked Arnie.

Arnie pointed at Eddie again. "I said she's a guy."

The creases on Joe's forehead deepened. "You're telling me that the woman I love is a guy?"

Arnie nodded.

Pow! Joe punched Arnie in the face so hard the big guy fell backwards.

"*You get out of my sight!*" Joe screamed at him. "*If I ever see you again, I'll kill you!*"

"But—" Arnie whimpered, holding his jaw.

Joe made another fist. "*You heard me!*"

Arnie scrambled to his feet and disappeared

out the door. Joe went back to Eddie. "I'm sorry, honey," he said. "I hope that big jerk didn't hurt your feelings."

Eddie just shook his blond curls.

"I never realized how dumb that guy was," Joe muttered. "If he can't see that you're a hundred and ten percent total female."

Frank rolled his eyes and turned away so that Joe wouldn't see the big smile on his face.

Meanwhile, Brian cleared his throat and clapped his hands together. "Ahem. Okay, band, it's time to go on again!"

THE NEXT MORNING, FRANK GOT UP early. Eddie walked with him to the bus station. The rest of the band was still asleep. Neither of them was dressed like a girl, but Frank carried his makeup and girl clothes in a bag.

"You sure you'll be back in time for the gig tonight?" Eddie asked.

"Yeah. The bus ride's only two hours," Frank said. "I'll be back by eight."

"Good. We need you, dude."

Frank glanced at him. "You sure you want to stick with this?"

Eddie looked surprised. "Stick with the band? Of course."

"But you're not a girl, Eddie."

Eddie's eyes grew large and he pressed a finger to his lips. "Hey, keep it down, okay? The Femme Brigade are gonna be stars, dude. We're cuttin' records and goin' on tours. This is the break we've dreamed of all our lives. We've fooled everyone this long. There's no way we're quittin' now."

Frank just stared at him and shook his head. "And what about Sharkbait Joe?"

"Don't worry about him," Eddie said. "I've got him eating out of the palm of my hand."

"Aren't you worried he may find out you're not a girl?" Frank asked.

Eddie shook his head and batted his eyes. "Believe me, Frankie, he's gonna think I'm a girl for a long time," he said in his Ellie voice. He put a hand on his hip and bent the other hand daintily. "I'm getting good at this."

The Clam Shanty was one of those huge places on the shore with a parking lot the size of a football field and a million tables covered with red and white checked plastic tablecloths. It was the kind of place where waiters and waitresses worked hard, scurrying around lugging huge aluminum trays piled high with clams, lobsters, and shrimp rolls.

It was mid-morning by the time Frank arrived. The place was still empty and the waiters and waitresses, all wearing red and white Clam Shanty T-shirts and red shorts, were just arriving to get ready for the lunch shift.

Frank sat down in a booth. He was wearing sunglasses and a baseball cap pulled down low. A few moments before, he'd tipped the maitre d' five dollars and asked him to seat him at a table Sabrina covered.

Now she came toward him wearing her uniform and carrying a pad of paper.

"Can I help you?" she asked.

"What's good?" Frank asked, disguising his voice and looking down at the table so she couldn't see his face.

"It really depends on what you want," Sabrina said.

"Oh, just something warm and comforting," Frank said.

"How about some clam chowder?"

"Sounds good," Frank said.

Sabrina left to get him his chowder. A little while later she returned with a steaming bowl.

"Here you go," she said, sliding the bowl in front of him. She started to turn away.

"Hey, didn't you used to sing with that all-girl band?" Frank asked without looking up.

Sabrina stopped and looked back at him. She nodded.

"What happened?" Frank asked.

Sabrina shrugged. "It didn't work out." She started to turn away again.

"Sorry to hear that," Frank said. "You know, I play in a band."

Sabrina walked a few steps and then stopped and looked back at him with a funny expression on her face.

"Oh?"

Frank nodded. "Yeah. They're called the Femme Brigade. You haven't heard of them yet, but they're gonna be real big."

Sabrina blinked and took a step back toward the booth. "Aren't they an all-girl band?"

"Yeah."

Sabrina took a step closer. "You're not a girl."

"Depends on who you ask."

Sabrina slid in next to him in the booth. She reached toward him and lifted the sunglasses off his face.

"Not if you ask me," she said, tracing his face with her fingertips. Her eyes started to fill with tears, but they were tears of happiness.

"I hope so," Frank said. "Because your opinion's the only one I really care about."

Sabrina threw her arms around his neck and kissed him. Frank put his arms around her and held her tight. Around the restaurant, the other waiters and waitresses stopped what they were doing and stared. But Frank didn't care. The only thing that mattered was Sabrina.

Because she was the one.

And now she was his.

TODD STRASSER has written many award-winning novels for both adults and teenagers. Several of his works have been adapted for the screen, including *Workin' for Peanuts*, *A Very Touchy Subject*, and *The Accident*, which he adapted himself. A former newspaper reporter and advertising copywriter, Strasser worked for several years as a television scriptwriter on such shows as *The Guiding Light*, *Tribes*, and *Riviera*.

In addition to writing, Strasser speaks frequently at schools about the craft of writing and conducts writing workshops for young people. The author of more than fifty novels, Strasser lives with his family in a suburb of New York City.